-194

# Troubled Journey

### Mysteries by Richard Lockridge

TROUBLED JOURNEY
A RISKY WAY TO KILL
DIE LAUGHING
A PLATE OF RED HERRINGS
MURDER IN FALSE-FACE

WITH OPTION TO DIE
MURDER FOR ART'S SAKE
SQUIRE OF DEATH
MURDER CAN'T WAIT
MURDER ROUNDABOUT

### Other Books by Richard Lockridge

ONE LADY, TWO CATS
A MATTER OF TASTE

THE EMPTY DAY
ENCOUNTER IN KEY WEST

MR. AND MRS. NORTH

## Books by Frances and Richard Lockridge
### Cats

CATS AND PEOPLE

### Mr. and Mrs. North

MURDER BY THE BOOK
MURDER HAS ITS POINTS
THE JUDGE IS REVERSED
MURDER IS SUGGESTED
THE LONG SKELETON
VOYAGE INTO VIOLENCE
DEATH OF AN ANGEL
A KEY TO DEATH
DEATH HAS A SMALL VOICE
CURTAIN FOR A JESTER
DEAD AS A DINOSAUR
MURDER COMES FIRST
THE DISHONEST MURDERER

MURDER IS SERVED
UNTIDY MURDER
DEATH OF A TALL MAN
MURDER WITHIN MURDER
PAYOFF FOR THE BANKER
KILLING THE GOOSE
DEATH TAKES A BOW
HANGED FOR A SHEEP
DEATH ON THE AISLE
MURDER OUT OF TURN
A PINCH OF POISON
THE NORTHS MEET MURDER
MURDER IN A HURRY

### Captain Heimrich

THE DISTANT CLUE
FIRST COME, FIRST KILL
—WITH ONE STONE
SHOW RED FOR DANGER
ACCENT ON MURDER
PRACTISE TO DECEIVE
LET DEAD ENOUGH ALONE
BURNT OFFERING

DEATH AND THE GENTLE BULL
STAND UP AND DIE
DEATH BY ASSOCIATION
A CLIENT IS CANCELED
FOGGY, FOGGY DEATH
SPIN YOUR WEB, LADY!
I WANT TO COME HOME
THINK OF DEATH

### Mystery Adventures

THE DEVIOUS ONES
QUEST OF THE BOGEYMAN
NIGHT OF SHADOWS
THE TICKING CLOCK
AND LEFT FOR DEAD
THE DRILL IS DEATH

THE GOLDEN MAN
MURDER AND BLUEBERRY PIE
THE INNOCENT HOUSE
CATCH AS CATCH CAN
THE TANGLED CORD
THE FACELESS ADVERSARY

# Richard Lockridge

# Troubled
## ∾ Journey

J. B. Lippincott Company

*Philadelphia and New York*

1970

The lyrics quoted on pages 83 and 85 are from
"Love's the Shortest Distance Between Two People,"
copyright 1954 by Mark Bucci and Hildegarde
Dolson, and are reprinted with the permission of the
authors.

A condensed version of this novel has appeared in
*Good Housekeeping.*

For Hildy ✎

# Troubled Journey

# 1 ∾

It was a cold, gray morning. The coldness and fog of the morning lay in her mind. She had hoped for sunshine; it was a bad day to start so long a trip. It is almost the way it was before, she thought, and pushed that thought out of her mind. It held against her pushing.

It isn't that, she thought. It isn't that at all. It is merely a bad morning, and in late November one has to expect many mornings to be bad. It will be better tomorrow and the day after tomorrow, because I am driving toward the sun. Even later today it will be better. It is not the way it was before. It is the day itself, not my reaction to the day. It is a bad morning for everybody; the fog is in the air, not in my mind. It is not at all the way it was before.

It was too early for traffic to be thick on Fifth Avenue, as she drove the Buick south, her lights on against the fog. She drove slowly; it was not a day for driving fast. It would not be on the turnpike; on the turnpike warnings would glow faintly through the fog. "Speed Limit 45," the signs would warn.

She turned the knob of the radio and it buzzed for seconds, and a voice said, "And now the news, brought to you this morning by Dannon Yogurt. Heavy fog has forced curtailment of flights at all major airports. All flights into and out of Newark have been canceled. Delays in departures are reported by both Kennedy International and La Guardia, and

( 9 )

incoming flights are being diverted. However, the United States Weather Bureau expects conditions to improve by late morning. The full weather report may be heard later in this broadcast. In Washington, the senate's debate over the controversial nomination of Winston Clay is expected to resume shortly after ten this morning. The majority leader, Senator Brock, cautiously predicts a vote will be taken late next week. In Vietnam, sporadic fighting is reported in the Da Nang area, where North Vietnamese regulars continue—"

She cut the radio off. Fog was enough without Vietnam. She edged the Buick to the right and waited for a bus to trundle out of the way, and turned into Thirteenth Street. Thirteenth Street was full of trucks. The one in front of her hissed its brakes off and advanced ten feet, and its stop lights went on and she braked hard. In his harness, on his leash in the rear seat, Toby yowled. But he had been yowling, with only a few pauses to insert a moan, since Frank had slammed the trunk lid down in front of the apartment house in the mid-eighties and said, "All set, Mrs. Sanders. Have a nice trip," and she had hooked Toby to the staple installed for his benefit. Carol turned to speak to her indignant cat, to tell him that everything was going to be all right, but then the truck inched forward again and she turned back and inched after it. Toby, crouched on the back seat, yowled again, and she could feel the glare in his eyes.

She inched to Sixth Avenue and across it; she inched to Seventh with horns blaring around her—blaring exasperation and impatience and the conviction of drivers that all the cars and trucks ahead needed to do was to grind through the cars ahead of them.

It was better going down Seventh; it wasn't good, but it was better. The Holland Tunnel closed around her, hemmed her, but it always closed around her and clamped her inside itself. And, as always, she expected her car to stall, although it was a young car and had never stalled in its life. (Stall or blow a tire.) Carol Sanders's mornings were filled with forebodings.

But it's not the way it was before, she told herself, with

Toby yowling in the seat behind her. It's not at all the way it was before. I'm perfectly all right now. They all say I'm perfectly all right. It's just that I'm not a morning person. A lot of people feel low in the morning; feel shapeless anxiety in the morning, and unformed apprehension. It is only part of being a non-morning person. It hasn't anything to do with the way it was the other time.

Ahead there was a change of light—not a brightness, but light of a different texture. That was the end of the tunnel. That was the fog of New Jersey, which looked as thick as the fog of New York. She drove out into it and followed signs and stopped at a booth and ran the window down and took the ticket which ejected itself at her. Cold, damp air, acrid with the smell of oil, poured into the car. Toby didn't like that, either, and said so loudly. She ran the window up and closed warmth in for herself and her cat, who didn't want to be driven to Florida.

At first the entrance road to the New Jersey Turnpike was relatively clear of traffic. But then ahead it curved down, to join the turnpike itself, and the turnpike looked solid with cars, their lights dim in the fog. At first she thought that the massed cars were standing still, but then she realized that they were creeping forward. When she came to the massed cars she inched the Buick in among them—in behind a trailer truck. Another trailer towered on her left, and behind her a truck seemed to nibble at her bumper.

Wedged so, her speed set, enforced, by the speed of others, it seemed to her that she was driving much too fast— that she was locked in a dangerous speed, her windshield wipers clawing at grayness. I can't see, something in her mind said. *I can't see!*

She groped for levers which seemed to dodge away from her fingers. She found one—one that had to be the right one; one that had better be the right one—and pressed down on it. She did not dare to look at the dials. But warm air came out at her from the dash, and she knew that the lever she had pressed down on the panel had been the right lever and that now it stood opposite "Defrost." And after a time the

( 11 )

windshield cleared a little. She could see the back of what was ahead.

It was a great square and there was a window in the back. On either side small red flags swayed in the wet air. Between them, painted on a spread of canvas, were the words, "Wide Load." And under that, stenciled in script on a trailer's metal, was a hyphenated word—"Porto-Home."

Of all the things to be caught behind, she thought. Of all the *monstrous* things.

Then she heard the scream. It was as loud as if it sounded in her ears. As loud and as tortured. But it was a scream which sounded only in her mind. It was an echo of a scream; it was a remembered scream.

Involuntarily, she pressed down on the brake pedal. There was a high, harsh roar in the air then, as the truck behind blasted at her. She moved her foot to the gas pedal, and the Buick, which had barely checked the speed into which it was locked, moved up and took, again, its fixed place in a formulated world.

The scream still sounded in her mind. But then it faded, seemed to grow more distant. That was the way it had been before. Then it ended. As it had ended before.

# 2 ∽

He had been a quiet man in a gray suit—a lightweight grey suit, because it had been warm in mid-September. It had been almost hot that evening. When the doorbell rang she had been lying on a sofa in the living room, and Emma had been sitting beside her on a straight chair and saying, "There, Mrs. Sanders. He'll give you something to make it better, Mrs. Sanders. Just you lie still, Mrs. Sanders."

But she could not lie still. She moved on the sofa, twisted on the sofa. And Emma held her hand and said, "There, Mrs. Sanders. There, ma'am."

When the doorbell rang Emma had said, "There he is now. There's the doctor," and had gone—had almost run —out of the living room into the entrance corridor. But when she came back it was not with the doctor. It was with the man in the gray suit. The man said, "Detective Bronson, ma'am. I'm sorry to bother you, Mrs. Sanders." He had stopped then and looked at her, and she had tried to sit up on the sofa. "You are Mrs. Sanders?" the man in the gray suit said.

She was almost sitting up, but then she felt herself slipping back again. It was as if there were no muscles in her body; no bones to brace the muscles. She let herself slip back so that her head was again on the pillow. It wasn't where the pillow was supposed to be. It was a cushion, really. Not a pillow. It was part of the back of the sofa. Emma must have—

"Yes," she said. "I'm Mrs. Sanders. Mrs. Benjamin Sanders. He—?" She had meant it to be a question. It would have been a meaningless question.

"Yes, Mrs. Sanders," Detective Bronson said. "It was instantaneous."

"He screamed," she said. "I heard him scream. I heard him. I heard—"

"Yes," Bronson said.

He stood by the sofa and looked down at her. He said, "We have to ask about things like this," he said. "But I can come back later if that will make it easier." He turned to Emma and said, "She ought to have a doctor. Somebody with her."

"I'm with her, mister," Emma said. "And I've called a doctor. The poor lady."

Bronson sat down in the chair Emma had been sitting in. It was, she thought muzzily, almost as if this man in a gray suit, this quiet man, were himself a doctor. Bronson said, "We have to find out what happened, Mrs. Sanders. We have to make a report. But there isn't any hurry about it. I can go and come back. Or somebody can come back."

"I don't know," she said. "I heard the scream. It—it went on and on. And then—and then it stopped."

"Yes," Bronson said. "That's the way it—" He paused. He said, "You were in the room, Mrs. Sanders? Saw him—fall? It wasn't this room."

"The kitchen," she said. "The big window in the kitchen. No, I didn't—I didn't see him at the window. I was in my own room. I was dressing. We'd—we'd been going out to dinner with friends. I thought he was in his own room changing. We—she'd asked us to dress. I was starting to put lipstick on when I heard it. It—it didn't sound like Ben. But it seemed to come from the kitchen. I ran there. I think that was the way it was. I think that was the way it was."

"I'm sorry, Mrs. Sanders," the man in the gray suit said. "If it's too much for you I can come back. Or somebody can come back. We have to find out how things like this happened. That's the way things are set up."

"You ought," Emma said, "to leave the poor lady alone at a time like this."

He turned and looked up at her.

"Ferguson," she said. "I'm Emma Ferguson. I work for the—I work for Mrs. Sanders. I've got a room downstairs. It goes with this apartment. That is, they own it too. It's—"

"Yes," Bronson said. "I understand the setup, Mrs. Ferguson. Mr. Harris filled me in. Says he called up here first. After he'd called the police, that is. And that there wasn't any answer and he called you. Because he'd seen Mrs. Sanders looking down from the window and knew she was here and—"

"The poor lady fainted," Emma said. "Anybody would faint, Mr. Bronson. And I came right up and she was lying in here and I got her up on the sofa and—"

To Carol it seemed as if they were talking from a long way off, and about something she did not understand. But then Bronson turned back to her and said, "You all right, Mrs. Sanders? Up to telling me what happened? If you're not—"

"I know," she said. "You told me you'd go away and come back. Or somebody would come."

"There has to be a report," Bronson said. "It's the way things are."

"I was sitting at my dressing table," she said. "I was putting a face on because we were going out. And then I heard this screaming. It—it was awful. And I thought it came from the kitchen and I—I called my husband and he didn't answer and—I ran out to the kitchen because that was where the screaming seemed to be. It's—show him where the kitchen is, Emma. He'll want to see where the kitchen is."

"Later," Bronson said, "I'll look around later, Mrs. Sanders. Get the lay of things. You went to the kitchen. And?"

"The window was open. Mostly it isn't opened because of the air conditioning. We've still got it on because it's been so warm."

"Yes," Bronson said. "The window was open."

"The curtains were blowing a little," she said. "I didn't hear the screaming any more so—so I looked down. There was—there was something—something on the ground. All huddled up. And—I hate to look so far down. I didn't want to live so high up because I'm afraid when I look down."

"A good many people are, Mrs. Sanders," Bronson said. He spoke gently.

"But Ben had this apartment for years before I met him," Carol said. "So when we were married we moved in here."

"I understand," Bronson said. "You looked down. Saw—well, what you saw. And then?"

"Mr. Harris came out," she said. "He's the superintendent."

"Yes."

"He came running out. He lives on the first floor. In the rear. There's a door down there to the areaway. He—he ran over to—to Ben's body. That was what I saw, wasn't it? Ben's body?"

"Yes. It was Mr. Sanders's body."

"He looked up. Mr. Harris, I mean. I was—I was leaning out of the window and looking down and he looked up and saw me. Then he ran back into the building and I—I must have come back in here. I don't remember. And then Emma said, 'You're all right, Mrs. Sanders. There's been a bad accident, but you're all right.' Something like that."

"You'd fainted," Emma Ferguson said. "And no wonder. And I got you up on the sofa and put a cold cloth on your head."

"I don't remember," Carol said. "I—the last thing I remember is looking down and seeing Mr. Harris go back into the building. That's all I remember, Mr. Bronson. You did say it was 'Bronson,' didn't you?"

"Yes," he said. "It's Bronson."

He stood up, then. He said, "I'm sorry I've had to put you through this, Mrs. Sanders. You've been brave about it. The doctor'll give you something, probably." He stopped but continued to look down at her.

"One more thing I've got to ask you," he said. "Always

have to ask about it. Had your husband been well lately? Going to see a doctor or anything like that?"

She tried to sit up again. This time she made it. But she held on, with both hands, to the arm of the sofa. She looked up at the quiet detective.

"He was always very well," she said, and her voice changed. It became more decisive. "There wasn't anything like what you're implying. It—it was an accident. He was opening the window and lost his balance."

"Yes," Bronson said. "That's probably the way it was. No reason to think it was any other way. You just rest now, Mrs. Sanders."

He turned to Emma Ferguson and said, "Mind showing me where the kitchen is, Mrs. Ferguson? Have to get the layout clear in my mind."

"If it's all right with Mrs. Sanders," Emma said.

Carol nodded her head. She leaned against the back of the sofa but continued to hold on, with both hands, to the sofa's arm. She sat so for what seemed a long time, and then Bronson came back and stood in the doorway which led to the entrance hall.

"Sorry to have had to bother you," Bronson said. "Probably won't have to again."

"It's all right," Carol said.

"You ought to have somebody with you," he said.

"Emma will be here," she told him. "I'll be all right."

She started to stand up, but when she did she was dizzy. She sat back on the sofa and held with both hands to the sofa arm.

"I'll take care of her," Emma Ferguson said. "I'll put her to bed and stay with her. I'll—"

The doorbell interrupted. This time it was the doctor. It was Dr. Strom. Dr. Strom's office was only a block or two away. But Dr. Strom didn't visit his patients. His patients went to him, stayed an hour with him; made appointments for the next hour with him. There are cobwebs in my mind, she thought. Dr. Strom is a cobweb in my mind. Wait—no. His name is in my address book. Under "D" for "doctor."

( 17 )

His name was the only name under "D" for doctor. That was how Emma—

"How do you feel?" Dr. Strom said and sat on the chair Bronson had sat on. "Pretty down? It's a good deal to take."

"I'll be all right," Carol said. "It won't come back."

Strom was in his late fifties. He was not a tall man. He had thick gray hair, but he did not have a beard. Two years ago when she had first gone to his office she had expected him to have a beard. She had expected him to speak with an accent. That was the way they were on TV and in movies. They had beards and spoke with—

"No," Strom said. "It won't come back, Mrs. Sanders. You'll ride it out, my dear. Shock now, of course. But that will wear off. You feel a little vague, probably. Is that the way you feel?"

"I guess so," she said. "Everything seems—seems a long way off. My husband's dead, doctor. Did somebody tell you my husband's dead? That he fell out of a window?"

"Yes," Strom said. "Somebody told me, Mrs. Sanders."

He reached down and opened the bag he had put on the floor beside his chair.

"And," he said, "that you fainted. Fell, apparently. Bang yourself up at all?"

"I don't think so."

"Probably eased down," Strom said. He took a hypodermic out of his bag and opened a vial and put the needle in the liquid in the vial. She watched him; watched his slow, careful movements. It was somehow as if she repeated his slow movements. He left the needle in the vial and reached out and put a finger on her right wrist. He had strong, hard fingers.

He held a finger on her pulse for some seconds, but did not use his watch to time the beats. He said, "Fine. Couldn't be better," and took his hand from her wrist and took the hypodermic out of the vial it rested in. She thought, Sterilizing. Of course that's it. They always—

He pushed the needle through the cork of another vial

and when he took it out again there was liquid in the tube of the hypodermic.

"Make you quiet," he said. "Let you sleep. Hold out your arm, my dear."

She held her arm out and he rubbed damp gauze on a place on her arm, and then there was the sharp sting of the needle.

"There we are," Strom said and took the needle out of her arm. "You'll do, my dear." He turned in his chair and looked up at Emma Ferguson. He said, "You're the one who called me?"

"Emma," she said. "Mrs. Emma Ferguson. I work for Mrs. Sanders."

"Good," the doctor said, and got up. "You'll get her to bed? Stay with her tonight?"

"I certainly will," Emma said. She was a little belligerent about it. "Think I'd just go away and leave her?"

"No," Strom said. "She'll be all right. Call me in the morning. Or she can. But she'll be fine." He turned back to Carol Sanders. "Hear that?" he said. "You'll be fine. It won't come back. Make an appointment if you'd like to. Next week some time. But only if you want to. There's no real need."

"Maybe—" she said, but already she felt herself sinking into softness. When Emma came back from letting the doctor out she said, "Can't I stay right here, Emma?"

"No," Emma said, "you can't, Mrs. Sanders. Bed is the place for you."

Emma held out both hands, and Carol Sanders took them and was pulled to her feet.

It was beginning to get light when she wakened, and for seconds she did not remember. But then memory came back, as if somebody had drawn open a blind and, for a second, she heard the scream again. Then Emma Ferguson came into the room with a tray, and the smell of coffee came into the room. Emma put the tray down beside her and went across the bedroom and opened curtains, and the sun came in . . .

There were things to do, then. For several days there were

things to do—things that almost filled the days. There were telegrams to send—telegrams to Mr. and Mrs. Wilbur Hudson in Vero Beach, because Maude Hudson was Benjamin Sanders's sister; a telegram to Mr. and Mrs. Felix Sanders because Felix was Ben's brother. The telegram to the Sanderses could not be delivered to Vero Beach, because the Sanderses were in Europe. There were telephone calls to answer and calls to make. One of the calls to make was to Ursula Fields, advertising manager of Bryant & Washburn, on Fifth Avenue. Ursula said, "Of course, dear. We all read about the dreadful thing. Come back whenever you feel up to it. There'll always be a place for you here. You know that."

There had not been much to read about it in the *Times* or in the *Post* or in the *Daily News*. "Benjamin Sanders, president of the Porto-Homes Corporation, fell to his death yesterday from a window of his tenth-floor apartment on upper Fifth Avenue. His death is listed by the police as accidental. Porto-Homes, which Mr. Sanders headed, manufactures house trailers and has plants in Connecticut, Florida and California."

A good many people fall (or jump) from high windows in New York City. If they do not, for hours, hesitate on ledges while firemen string nets below them and policemen and clergymen and psychiatrists plead with them, they rate names and ages and bare facts in type. Benjamin Sanders had been forty-two years old when he fell (or jumped) from a tenth-floor window.

Bodies must be put in coffins, even if they are to be burned. Coffins must be chosen by survivors, from spreading rooms of coffins, available at various prices. The price of a coffin includes that of other services. A clergyman of the proper denomination must be employed. Maude Hudson, who flew up from Vero, decided that. "We've always been Episcopalians." She also went with Carol to the display of coffins, and it was she who decided which would be suitable. It was she who found out when the authorities would release the body for burial after the autopsy which the circumstances of death made necessary. It was she who sat beside Carol on a hard bench in a big, almost empty, undertaker's chapel while a robed priest of the Episcopal Church read words from a little book—words mercifully few and formal. Maude was a woman to be relied on, like an older sister.

She had a rather long, lean face, with specific bones; except that her eyes were blue, as Benjamin's had been, she did not resemble her brother, who had been a tall man and a little inclined to be a heavy man. Maude was only an inch or two taller than Carol's own five feet two. Together on the hard bench they had been two small black figures. When the ritual of the service had required that they stand, Maude had taken Carol's arm and helped her up, although by then Carol Sanders did not need to be helped to stand.

The day after the funeral, Carol rode with her sister-in-law to Kennedy International. It was still warm that day, although a little hazy. Maude's plane for Jacksonville, where she would change for a Vero plane, was only half an hour late in taking off.

They talked little in the cab which took them to Kennedy, but it seemed to Carol that Maude, sitting beside her, was intent, as if she were planning to say something of importance. She did not say anything of importance. She said, as she had said several times before, that Bill had been terribly upset that he couldn't come up with her to help with things. And that he just couldn't, couldn't get away from the plant. Particularly when there were so many loose ends and with Felix off in some remote place—some tiny little place—in Italy.

Felix Sanders had answered his sister's cable, but only after almost two days. He had said, "Trying to make reservations. Difficult this time of year." And he had cabled Carol: "Our deepest sympathy. Vinnie and Felix."

It was only after her flight had been announced that Maude Hudson got to the point which, Carol suspected, she had been considering during the long, slow ride from upper Fifth to what had begun during it to seem the other end of nowhere.

Maude Hudson had stopped at the gate and turned to Carol and said, "I hate to leave you here alone, dear. What will you do? You can't stay alone in that big apartment."

"I don't know yet," Carol said. "I really haven't thought yet."

"I do know about this job of yours," Maude said. "The one that seems to mean so much to you. The job you kept on with even after you and Ben were married."

"Ben had to be away a good deal on business," Carol said, and felt that, somehow, there was a defensive inflection in her voice. But Ben had never objected to her continuing as a junior copy writer in the advertising department of Bryant & Washburn's.

"It's not as if you need to have a job," Maude said, and others bound for the plane went past them. They made an eddy in a stream. "For the money, I mean. Not now. And not after you and Ben were married, of course."

"It wasn't the money," Carol said. "Not after we were married, anyway. It's—it's just something I like doing. Something I was getting—well, to be rather good at. But I don't know what I'll do, Maude. Hadn't you better—?"

"Goodness," Maude said. "I certainly had." She started to walk after the now-diminished stream of passengers for the Jacksonville plane. But after a few steps she stopped and turned back. She had to raise her voice a little.

"Come down to Vero," she called to Carol. "That's what you ought to do. Not stay up here alone in the cold. Look— I'll have Ben's house—your house now—got ready and you—"

"I'll think about it," Carol called back to her. "*Maude!* You must get on your plane."

Maude Hudson turned and began to walk fast, began almost to run, toward the big jet. Carol watched. Her sister-in-law was the last to go up the ramp. The plane waddled through a turn and went off toward the end of a runway, making a great noise about it.

Carol had to wait fifteen minutes for a cab to take her

( 22 )

back to Manhattan, and it took a long time to get to upper Fifth Avenue.

In the apartment, which seemed big for her—big and empty—she took off the black dress and put on a tawny one of lightweight wool, although it was warm enough that September day for summer clothes. She felt better in the gayer dress. The black dress of mourning had seemed, somehow, a pretense, almost a masquerade. And Tobermory, sleek and talkative, like the famous cat he had been named for, came out from under a bed and jumped on her lap. Most of the time Maude Hudson had stayed in the apartment he had spent under beds.

Toby had got himself settled when the telephone rang. He leaped away and ran toword the telephone, talking at the top of his Siamese voice. He always ran to answer the telephone. Once he had run under Ben's feet when Ben was going to do his own answering. Ben had sworn at him and brushed him out of the way with a foot. He had not really, Carol thought, kicked her cat. You couldn't call it kicking. Toby had thought it was and had snarled about it. Not that it wasn't what he expected of this large human who had intruded on an ordered life.

Carol said, "Be quiet, Toby," and lifted the receiver and said, "Hello?" She agreed that she was Mrs. Sanders.

"Detective Bronson, Mrs. Sanders. Wonder if I could come around and see you when it's convenient? Couple of small points I'm supposed to get cleared up."

She said, "Today, Mr. Bronson?"

"If it's convenient. Say in about an hour?"

"I was just—" she said and then, "All right. In about an hour."

"Shouldn't take long," Bronson said, and clicked off.

It was then a little after noon. She had been thinking of going out—going out very much alone—for lunch. But it didn't matter. Emma had been told not to bother about lunch, because there was no certainty about the time which would be needed to see Maude Hudson off. But there was always food. Emma Ferguson saw to that.

( 23 )

Carol made herself a drink, and Toby came to her lap to help her drink it. She finished and lifted Toby down and went down the long corridor to the kitchen—went past the open door to her bedroom and the closed door of the room which had been Ben's. She made herself a sandwich and coffee and carried a tray back to the living room. Toby was a tight curl of cat in a corner of a sofa. Toby had had lunch.

She had finished the sandwich and carried empty cup and empty plate to the kitchen, she had gone back to the living room and lighted a cigarette, when the doorbell rang. It had been almost exactly an hour. Detective Bronson wore the same gray suit, and he was sorry to have to bother her. He said there was always a lot of routine; always a lot of forms which had to be filled out. He chose a straight chair, and she sat opposite him in a lower, more comfortable, chair after he had said thanks, but that there wasn't anything she could offer him.

"The other day," Bronson said, "you said your husband had been well recently. Hadn't gone to a doctor or anything like that. The way you remember it, Mrs. Sanders?"

She said, "Yes, Mr. Bronson."

"Of course," Bronson said, "I suppose he could have been going to a doctor without telling you. Not wanting to worry you."

"He didn't—" she said, but did not finish. She said, "Yes, I suppose he could. I was at my office most days and of course he was at his. And he often had to go up to the plant for a day or two."

"Sure," Bronson said. "I see how it is, Mrs. Sanders. You and he'd been married about how long?"

"About a year." She checked her mind. "A little over a year. A year ago last July."

"He hadn't changed during the year? I mean, in his attitudes."

She said she didn't know quite what he meant.

"In his behavior," Bronson said. "In the way he acted. Not—oh, jumpy? Apt to fly off the handle? That sort of thing? As if something was, call it eating him?"

She did not answer for a moment. Then she said, "Why are you asking these things, Mr. Bronson? What makes you think he'd changed?"

He did not answer that. He said, "He hadn't been inclined to get angry about nothing in particular? Or, to forget things? Kind of lose his way?"

She shook her head.

"Perfectly rational?"

"Is anybody?" she said. "All the time?"

"No," Bronson said. "I guess not, Mrs. Sanders. Recently, had your husband seemed depressed?"

"Oh," she said, "sometimes. Nobody's on top of the world all the time. You—all right. I do know what you're getting at. Was he sick? Mentally sick? And because he was, killed himself? That's what you're talking about, isn't it?"

"We just like to get the record straight," Bronson said. "Rather a high sill the kitchen window has. Not one of these low ones you might fall over if, say, you got sort of dizzy."

"You do think he committed suicide? Because—because he was sick?"

"It's possible," Bronson said. "Because, the point is, Mrs. Sanders, he was sick. Showed up in the autopsy. He had a brain tumor. Might have been operable, the pathologist says, but it would have been touch and go. He kept that from you?"

She did not say anything for several seconds. When she did speak her voice was very low and Bronson leaned a little toward her. She said, "I didn't know."

Bronson continued to lean toward her and seemed to wait.

"It was because of that," she said. "I—I didn't know."

"What was because of that?"

"You asked me before," Carol said. "I—it seemed like saying bad things about him. But—all right. Sometimes, in the last few months, he'd seemed strange. Not like himself. Not the way he was when—when we were first married. Before we were married. Easily excited. When there wasn't anything to be excited about. I don't know. Jumpy." At the word she put her hands up to cover her face. "I didn't mean to say that," she soid, and Bronson could hardly hear the muffled words. "It was—it was a hideous thing to say."

"Word people use all the time," Bronson said. "No reason to worry about having used it, Mrs. Sanders. What the pathologist said. This tumor would have—how did he put it? —resulted in personality changes. And your husband had to see a doctor about it, Mrs. Sanders. A doctor named—" He stopped as if he were trying to find a name lost in his mind, but she did not think he really was. "Strom," he said. "That's it. Isaac Strom. Psychoanalyst or something like that."

"Dr. Strom's a psychiatrist," she said. "A—a medical doctor. He uses psychoanalysis in therapy. Most of them do. But he's a doctor. Actually, he's a neurosurgeon. A doctor can have more than one specialty, you know. He's—"

She had taken her hands away from her face and was looking at Bronson and had leaned forward a little in her deep chair.

"I'm not telling you anything you don't know, am I?" she said, and her voice was clear, demanding.

"No," Bronson said. "Dr. Strom's pretty well known, Mrs. Sanders. To you too, apparently."

"My husband had been to see him," she said. "And—and knew what was the matter?"

"Yes," Bronson said. "Picked it up at your husband's office, Mrs. Sanders. Very cooperative they were there. His secretary had made an appointment for him about three weeks ago. With Dr. Strom. And after that he wasn't at the office for two, three days."

"Three weeks ago," Carol said, "he was up at the plant. Oh, most of the week. At least, he told me—"

She stopped. There wasn't any point in telling this man in a gray suit what Ben had told her.

"In a hospital," Bronson said. "Seems there are a lot of tests they have to make. Didn't want to worry you, Mrs. Sanders. Why he didn't tell you."

"You've seen Dr. Strom?"

"Yes," Bronson said. "Oh, yes, Mrs. Sanders. As soon as we got things put together. The doctor'd told your husband there'd have to be an operation. And that he couldn't guarantee anything. That his chances wouldn't be better than fifty-fifty. Doesn't seem to beat about the bush, this Strom. Only, maybe he did a little. Told us more. Told us Mr. Sanders's chances wouldn't have been as good as that, actually."

She said, "Ben. Poor Ben. And I thought—" She stopped. "But why didn't Dr. Strom—" She stopped again.

"He didn't tell you about the tumor? When he came to see you?"

Carol stared at Bronson. "He told you he came to see me?"

"Oh, no. Wouldn't have, that is. But I was still here when he came to see you, Mrs. Sanders. He came in as I went out, that evening."

Carol remembered sitting on the sofa, fighting dizziness. And then Dr. Strom . . . "He said shock," she said, "and gave me a shot." She groped. "It was so soon," she said. "He must have thought that just death—accidental death— was enough for me to take without the—without evidence of suicide."

"How long had you been his patient, Mrs. Sanders?"

"Oh, I wasn't really—not any more. I had been before I was married," she said. "For a few months. I—oh, I got to feeling sort of fuzzy. Didn't seem to track. And—and got to crying a lot. Mrs. Fields said I'd better go see somebody, and suggested Dr. Strom."

He didn't ask about Mrs. Fields. Perhaps, she thought, he's already asked Mrs. Fields about me.

He said, "When was this, Mrs. Sanders?"

"Two years ago," she said. "About two years ago. I was just starting at the office—I write advertising copy, Mr. Bronson—and it—well, I thought for a while it was going to be too much for me. That I'd never make the grade. It's—it's a straining sort of work, Mr. Bronson. You—sometimes you just get baffled. Especially when you're first starting. Trying to keep up."

"You saw Dr. Strom several times? And—he straightened things out for you?"

"For a little over two months," she said. "Once a week.

( 27 )

Yes, he straightened things out for me. He's—he's a very gentle, good man, Mr. Bronson. It was what they call a mild depression. Not really that, actually, but perhaps the start of one. And people come out of mild depressions, almost always, even if they don't go to doctors. And understanding about it, having things explained to me I—well, I felt all right again. And he said I'd go on feeling all right."

"You certainly seem all right to me," Bronson said. "Very level-headed young woman, I'd say. Going through a bad time, and doing fine about it. This—this mild-depression thing. Before you married Mr. Sanders?"

"Before I even met him."

"You tell him about it?"

"Yes. I—when I first met him I wanted him to know all about me."

"He took it all right? I mean, he wasn't worried?"

"He told me not to worry my head about it."

He had said, ". . . your pretty head, your lovely head." She could hear the words from a time which seemed very distant. But she did not repeat the words to Detective Bronson.

Then suddenly she thought, He found out that I've been Dr. Strom's patient; he—he thought, thinks, I may be crazy. *Crazy enough to push my husband out a window.* That's why he's come back again.

"Well," Bronson said, "I guess that about covers the ground, Mrs. Sanders. Sorry to have had to bother you again."

He stood up and looked down at her. He said, "By the way, you're not planning to go any place in the next few weeks?"

She stood up suddenly to face him. She said, "What you're saying is, I can't go any place. That's what you're saying, isn't it?"

"No," Bronson said. "You can go any place you like, of course. What makes you think you can't, Mrs. Sanders? Nothing I've said."

"Not in so many words," she said. "Not in—not in words at all."

"No reason to get notions," Bronson said. "No reason I know of, anyway. Probably won't have to bother you again at all. Only, might be some little detail for the records. We'd like to be able to get in touch with you if something comes up."

He began to move toward the hallway to the apartment door.

"My sister-in-law wants me to go down to Vero Beach," Carol said. "Where she and her husband and my brother-in-law—"

She paused for a moment. Then she said, "Will that be all right with the police?"

"You're jumpy," Bronson said. "Reason enough to be. Of course it will be all right with the police. Good time to go south. You think you will go?"

"I don't know yet," she said.

"If you decide to," Bronson said, "I'd appreciate it if you'd give me a ring. Tell me where you'll be. That sort of thing. O.K.? So if we want to get in touch."

"Have I got a choice?"

"All the choice in the world, Mrs. Sanders," Bronson said. "Just appreciate it if you'd call and tell us where you'll be. Mind writing the number down?"

He gave her a telephone number, and she wrote it down.

# 3 ∾

Bronson had not come back. For more than a week after the day he had given her the number to call she had answered her telephone each time with uneasiness, expecting the voice which answered hers to be Bronson's voice; expecting to be told that there were one or two points he'd like to clear up, for the record. But the voice which answered her "Hello?" had never been Bronson's. Nor had anybody else from the police called, although, in bad moments, she had thought that somebody might, to tell her not to leave town. She had heard, or read, that the police said that when they suspected people.

Gradually, the faint apprehension had dimmed. There were still many things to sign and many letters to answer and many things to be told about by Ben's lawyer. The chief of those things was about the will, in which everything Ben had owned—including the big apartment on upper Fifth—was left to her; was left to her with a proviso that the lawyer was slow in getting around to. Ben, it turned out, had owned a good deal, most of it in stock of the Porto-Homes Corporation.

The realizable value of that stock was not, the lawyer told her, easy to do more than guess at. Although technically "public," and listed on the American Exchange, the corporation was actually a closed one. "Your husband and his brother and sister owned all the stock," the lawyer told her.

"Or almost all of it. When we've gone through the formalities, gone through probate, you'll own a controlling interest, Mrs. Sanders. Meanwhile—I trust you have a bank account in your own name, Mrs. Sanders?"

"Yes," she said to that. "A few thousands. Almost everything was in our joint account. Ben arranged it that way after we were married."

"Yes," the lawyer said. "I've got his summary of that. Very careful about that sort of thing, your husband was. Only you can't draw against the joint account for the time being. You realize that? What they call 'the flag' is up. Account's blocked, until we've gone through probate and the tax people have made sure about their bite. Matter of months, probably. You'll be all right? Financially, I mean."

"I'll be all right."

The lawyer had a habit of putting the tips of his fingers together. He put them together then. He said, "Er." He added "Ah" to it. He said, "There's a rather—a rather curious provision in your husband's will, Mrs. Sanders. I, er, didn't like it when we drew the will up. Told Mr. Sanders so. This was a few months after you were married and—er."

He took his fingertips apart and clasped his hands and looked at her over them, across the desk. She said, "What is the provision?"

" 'All my property, real and personal, to my wife, Carol, provided she is not then under treatment for mental disorder. In the event that she is, I appoint my brother, Felix, to serve as her guardian until she is pronounced fully recovered by her physician, in consultation with such other qualified psychiatrist as my brother may select.' "

He folded the will up and slapped it gently on the desk top. He said, "Are you undergoing such treatment, Mrs. Sanders?"

"No," she said. "Could he do that?"

He said, "Mmm." He said, "Are your mother and father living, Mrs. Sanders? Or, say, brothers and sisters?"

"No. My parents died several years ago. I never had brothers or sisters."

( 31 )

"Have you any idea why your husband should have wanted this proviso in his will?"

"Before I met him, I'd been seeing a psychiatrist for a short time. I was—I was confused and depressed. But that didn't last, and it was a long time ago."

"You told Mr. Sanders about this, er, experience?"

"Yes. I didn't keep things from him."

"Of course not," the lawyer said. "Of course not." He put his fingertips together again. He nodded his head. "Makes the provision more understandable, I suppose," he said. "Keeps the control of the stock in the family in the event that, er."

"In case," Carol said, "I go bats. That's the word Dr. Strom used. He said, 'You're not going bats, my dear. Quit worrying.'"

The lawyer said, "Mmm." He said, "You haven't seen this psychiatrist, er, recently?"

"The day my husband died," Carol said, and spoke slowly and carefully, "Dr. Strom came to the apartment and gave me a shot so I could sleep. He came—oh, as a general practitioner might have come. Not as a psychiatrist."

"You haven't needed to see him since? For, er, other reasons?"

"Mr. Curtis," Carol said, "I'm entirely sane. As sane as you are." She managed to avoid adding, "At least." She did add, "As Dr. Strom will tell you."

"Fine," the lawyer said. "Nothing to worry about on these grounds, then."

He took papers out of the top drawer of his desk.

"Now," he said, "if you'll just sign these where I've put the 'X's.'"

"Being of sound mind," Carol said. He said, "Ha, very good," which Carol didn't, on the whole, think it was. She signed where the "X's" were.

"We'll be in touch," he said. He stood up behind his desk and held a hand across it. The hand, Carol thought, felt rather soft in her own slim, hard hand.

"By the way," he said, "I trust you have made your own will, Mrs. Sanders? Er, particularly now, that you are—or will be when we've got through the formalities—what they used to call a woman of property. Ha."

There is no reason to dislike a man because he says "Er" rather frequently and puts the tips of his fingers together, or because his handshake is a soft handshake. And it had not been he who had put that—that disturbing—proviso in the will. He had, in fact, questioned it. Or said he had.

"Yes," she said. "It—it was like my husband's." (Except there had been no proviso in it.) "Everything is to go to—" She stopped and then said, "Oh."

Not expectedly, Curtis said, "Er."

"Yes," Carol said, "I realize I'll have to make a new will, Mr. Curtis. I'll think about it."

She got out of the office, which had come to seem a stuffy office—almost a stifling office. When she got down to the street, wind was rushing through it, and it was not the balmy wind of the morning. But she walked the many blocks to her apartment, against the wind, and the words "provided she is not then under treatment for mental disorder" churned over and over in her mind.

And the next morning, which was the morning before she had arranged with Ursula Fields of Bryant & Washburn to go back to her desk there, she waked up with a cold. It turned out to be a bad cold, a cold which hung on and on, and she had not made it back to her desk. Even now, after so many weeks, the dregs of the cold drove toward the South with her on the New Jersey Turnpike—drove in November fog and the harsh air of diesel exhausts.

The police knew she was driving south. At least, she supposed they did. Two days before she drove down Fifth Avenue in the fog, she had dialed the number Bronson had given her. A man had said, "Detective Squad. Detective Wilson."

She had asked for Detective Bronson.

"Off today," Detective Wilson said. "Matter of fact—

wait a minute." She heard him call to somebody; called: "Larry's on leave, isn't he?" She heard a voice answer, but not the words.

"Detective Bronson's taking his vacation," Wilson told her. "Anything anybody else can do, ma'am?"

"I'm Mrs. Benjamin Sanders," she said. And was asked how to spell it. She spelled it. "I'm driving down to Vero Beach," she said. "In Florida. Mr. Bronson asked me to let him know if I left town. Let him know where I'd be."

"O.K.," Wilson said. "I'll pass it along. Vero Beach. Where in Vero Beach?"

She gave him details. He said, "Thanks, Mrs. Sanders. I'll see Detective Bronson gets the word."

Wilson had not seemed much interested. Her name apparently hadn't meant anything to him. Well, she had done what Bronson had asked her to do. He knew she was driving south, if anybody remembered to tell him.

For many miles she was hemmed in by trucks; for those many miles she seemed to rush forward in a box from which she could not escape. She felt always that she drove too fast, perilously too fast, with no control over her car's speed. But the speedometer hovered between forty and fifty. It was her powerlessness which made the speed seem great. The Porto-Home in front of her set her speed; the trucks thundering on her left held her from escape. She grew to hate the Porto-Home, although, in a sense, part of it was now her own.

Some time, she thought, it will turn off this road and trundle, heavily, to a lot somewhere. It will stop there and will be hooked to electric lines and telephone lines and piped, somehow, into water mains and sewers. And people— the people who have bought it—will live in it, tightly but secure.

She had never until she married heard of these movable houses, and when Ben had first told her what his business was—that he was "in" house trailers—she had thought of the trailers people hooked to the backs of their cars and hauled behind them to trailer camps. After their marriage,

Ben had taken her to see the Connecticut plant and the monsters which came out of it, and she had discovered that Porto-Homes were not the small objects which bobbed, often so uncertainly, behind family sedans. Porto-Homes were hauled by trucks and, at destinations, planted; there was nothing casual and nothing small about a Porto-Home. They were longer than any truck trailer had a right to be and by some feet wider. Their insides were the insides of houses, complete with everything and with everything compact and smooth and shining. Shown the inside of one at the plant, Carol had said they were perfectly wonderful, and marvelously efficient, and had wanted—had wanted with a kind of desperation—to get out.

"Everything a couple could need," Ben had told her. "And when they get tired of one part of the country they can get a truck—we rent them the trucks—and go some place else. It's a modern way of life." He had nodded his head. "We're building another plant in California. Now that they're building roads that will take them."

The Porto-Home ahead of Carol was taking more than its share of the road, and the New Jersey Turnpike is a wide road. For a long time there was nothing to do about it.

But beyond New Brunswick the fog began to lessen. After a time she was able to see again. And trucks, with a kind of reluctance, began to take exit roads from the turnpike. By the Hightstown exit, there was watery sunshine. She could drop back, then, until she could see around the Porto-Home. By then most of the trucks were in the outside lane.

She signaled and started to pull out, but a big bus beeped at her in anger and she went back behind the wide load. She tried again after a few miles and got into the center lane and pressed hard on the gas pedal. Even at seventy, the Porto-Home seemed interminable and seemed to be edging toward her. But finally she was past it. Because it was too soon to drive really fast, because her reflexes were not yet adjusted to speed, she cut back to the slow lane after the wide load was safely behind her. She left the fast lanes to those in a hurry.

The car behind followed her into the slower lane. Apparently its driver, too, felt himself not yet adjusted to turnpike speeds. She kept a little under sixty, which is slow for turnpike driving—where seventy is a norm, with glances at the mirror for patrol cars. The car behind was also content with a speed within the limit. It stayed behind; kept its conservative distance. On her left, cars, and not a few trucks, flashed past her. This afternoon, she thought, I will be confident again as these hurrying cars are confident; by tomorrow, certainly, I will be sure again.

The right front fender of the car behind was daubed with red paint. That's why he is cautious, Carol thought. Recently, he has crumpled his fender against something; he has daubed red paint on it to keep the rust out. His assurance, as well as his fender, has been dented.

As the sun brightened, her own confidence brightened with it. She did not quite give her little Buick—the light Buick with the big engine—its head. She had no precise idea what its head might be, except that the salesman, when she and Ben had gone together to buy it, had said that as far as he knew it would cruise contentedly enough at a hundred and twenty. He had added that he had, personally, no intention whatever of finding out. Carol, whose car it had become, knew only that at eighty it was still an eager little car. With the road wide and open ahead of it, as now this road was becoming, the little Buick was sly about its speed. It kept trying to go faster; if one was not attentive, sixty tended to become sixty-five and sixty-five to edge toward seventy.

She looked at her speedometer and the hand did show seventy. You cheat, Carol told her little car, and lessened pressure on the gas pedal. Unconsciously, she had spoken aloud. Toby answered her from the back seat and he was vehement. She risked a quick glance back. Toby was standing on his hind legs looking out a window. From his voice, he was not liking what he saw through the window.

"It's all right, Toby," Carol told her cat. "It goes by fast, but it won't hurt you. And you can't fall out because it's closed, and anyway your leash isn't long enough."

Toby liked to have things explained to him. When he spoke next she could tell that he was facing the back of her head. He sounded less angry; Toby was mollified when spoken to.

Carol said, "Good cat," to please him and kept her eyes on the road ahead, with frequent quick glances at the mirror. The car with the red-splashed fender was still about the same distance behind. Its driver, apparently, was fixing his speed to hers. He had not dropped back when the Buick, taking advantage of her absent-mindedness, had inched up to seventy.

The trucks ahead were spaced out, now. But, on a grade, she closed up rather rapidly on a tank truck. The side mirror showing nothing close, and she signaled and pulled out and went around the tank truck and, allowing more space than she needed, cut back to the outside lane. There she picked up speed to allow room for the car with the splashed fender, which had followed her around the tank truck and now followed her in front of it. The driver of the red-daubed car was losing his timidity. He was still letting her set the pace.

On long drives, and Carol had taken a good many, although none before in this eager little Buick, one grows familiar with certain cars. They stay behind one or in front of one; they pass and in turn are passed. A kind of companionship builds up and is broken, without hurt, when accustomed cars turn off on exit roads or, in towns, pull to curbs and stop. A station wagon with children wriggling and waving in the rear may be part of a pack for fifty miles, then be no longer, and never again, seen. There was nothing unusual about the same car following, keeping its set distance behind. She was conscious of this one merely because its blotched paint made it recognizable.

"Service Area, 1 Mile," a sign read. Beyond it a hundred yards or so there was another sign: "Next Service Area, 40 Miles."

Carol looked at her gas gauge. It showed the tank a quar-

( 37 )

ter full. Which might mean, which probably did mean, almost half full. The gauge had its own way of looking at things. Still—

When the access road showed ahead, she signaled for a right turn and drifted, slowing, toward the right. Before the curve hid the car behind, she saw it go on down the turnpike. Looking, she thought, for some other car to set its speed. She pulled up to one of a battery of pumps and waited, and a young man in a blue jacket with "Citgo" stenciled on it said, "Fill her up, miss?"

She said, "Yes. High test," and the young man disappeared behind the car. He reappeared after a grating sound. He said, "Check the oil, miss?" She said "Yes" to that. He began to clean the windshield. Toby growled at him, an intruder on private property. The young man stopped in mid-swipe and looked through glass at Toby. He said, "That a cat, miss?"

"Yes," Carol said. "He's Siamese."

"Doesn't sound like most cats," the young man said, and completed his wipe.

"They don't," Carol said. "Noisier."

"Sure are," the man said, and unlatched the hood and disappeared behind it. He came out and slammed the hood down and said, "All O.K., miss," and went to the rear and was gone for some seconds. He came back and said, "Five seventy-five, miss," and looked in, a little anxiously, at Toby. Toby said "Yah," in evident derision. The attendant shook his head and gave Carol change for a ten, and she ran her window up.

There was a Howard Johnson's in the service area and, although cars were clustered in its parking area, there did not seem impossibly many. Carol thought, Coffee would be a good idea, and circled into a marked oblong.

Sunshine was bright when she stepped out into it, and she got back into the car and lowered the rear windows a little so that Toby would have air. Even on a November day, with the sun slanting, glancing off, a car can get hot inside if windows are left closed. Toby said, "Yow-*oh*," and put his forepaws on the back of the front seat and watched her walk toward the restaurant.

"Just coffee, please," Carol told the counter waitress, who said, "Just coffee, miss?" and looked up at a clock, which said it was eleven-thirty. "Please, just coffee," Carol said and opened her handbag and took Maude Hudson's last letter out of it.

"We're so glad you're coming, dear," Carol read. "It will be so good for you to get out of that awful cold and everything. We'll have the house all ready for you and you can just sit on the beach and *soak* up sunshine. And all of us can get so many things settled."

That sentence puzzled Carol slightly, as it had a week before, after she had given up to the cold and told Ursula Fields that she really had to get out of New York's November dankness for, anyway, a few weeks and would call when she got back and see how things, and most particularly she, stood in the advertising department of Bryant & Washburn. "Get so many things settled?" What, precisely, had Maude meant by that? Conceivably about the stock of Porto-Homes, so much of which she now owned? But there was nothing to settle about that until Ben's will crept through surrogate's court. She could not sell it, if that was what Maude—and, of course, Felix Sanders—thought she might do. She couldn't vote it, if a vote was coming up. There would be, probably. The stockholders would have to elect somebody, obviously Felix, as president of the corporation to replace his dead brother. Probably that was all Maude had meant.

She skimmed on through Maude's letter, which was largely about how beautiful the weather had been all fall, except for a few days of hurricane, and how good it would be for Carol just to lie in their lovely sunshine. She skimmed to the second page and to what she had reread the letter to make sure about.

"When we drive," she read, "Bill and I always stop at the Stetson Motels. They're immaculate and there's always a passable restaurant near and you can always reserve one night for the next night and be *sure*." Maude, Carol had discovered, underlined a good many words in her letters. "And they'll take pets, so if you really decide to bring that dear cat of yours it will be all right. Most of them won't have pets, you know."

Carol had not known, and had been glad to be told. She had hesitated to go south partly because of Toby. Emma would, of course, have fed him and taken care of his toilet pan, but he wouldn't have liked being alone in the apartment. And Emma, after all she had done for so many weeks, had time off coming—time which would not include assiduous cat-sitting.

Carol said "Thank you" for a cup of coffee—and a glass of water and a napkin and a knife and fork, apparently to eat her coffee with. The coffee was hot and strong, and she sipped from the cup.

"If I were you," she read, "I'd stop at the first Stetson I came to and reserve for the night. As I remember, there's one in Delaware, a few miles after you cross the bridge at the end of the turnpike. They'll make a reservation for you at another Stetson a couple of hundred miles farther on, or however far you want to go, of course. If I were you, I'd follow the signs that say 'Bay Bridge' after that. There isn't *nearly* so much traffic that way and it keeps you out of Baltimore and everything. Unless it's Sunday. They say the bridge is *impossible* on weekends. Then—"

Carol did not finish with the careful instructions. She had already transferred them to a map. She drank her coffee and left her tip and paid at the desk. People were streaming into the restaurant as she went out of it.

Toby swore at her when she got into the car and started the motor. But there was relief in his profanity.

Traffic was light on the turnpike when she got back on it; it was already lunchtime for people driving south. She started to let the Buick have a part of its way and then a police car pulled out from the shoulder ahead of her and she slowed to the stipulated sixty.

A car which had been standing on the shoulder, behind

( 40 )

the cruise car, flicked its lights to show that it was—probably with a summons in its pocket—about to turn out from the shoulder. She touched the horn rim for warning and went past the car and, since the police car was vanishing rapidly ahead of her, probably at eighty, she let the little Buick have part of its way again.

There was little ahead of her on the sun-brightened highway and, in the mirror, little behind her. Then a car in her lane showed in the mirror, and it was closing rather rapidly. Which was, of course, no concern of hers. But then, as it drew closer, it was the car with the red-splotched right front fender.

When it was perhaps a quarter of a mile behind her it settled to her speed. And that was odd; vaguely, that was worrying. The car had not followed her into the service area, as she had half expected. It had gone on—by now it should have been twenty miles, or more than twenty miles, ahead of her. But, again, it was behind her.

Gone on beyond the service center? Gone too fast and been stopped by the patrol car? Conceivably the car she had tooted warning at when it seemed ready to turn out in front of her?

She thought that car had been a big black car. The car which had been so companionable for so many miles had been a big black car. Had the car which the police cruiser drove away from had red blotches on its right front fender? She had been on the wrong side of it to tell. Had it—had it parked to wait for her to get ahead of it? It is against the law to park at the side of the New Jersey Turnpike, except in the event of a breakdown, when cars wait for patrolling repair trucks and tie handkerchiefs to their radio antennas or signal by putting up the hoods. Had the patrol car stopped in front of the big black car merely to warn that only emergency stopping was lawful?

Carol curbed the Buick to sixty. The car behind kept its distance. But it had been a hurrying car; it had been gaining on her when her speed had been seventy. Now urgency had left it; now it was content to trail at sixty.

It doesn't mean anything, Carol told herself. It can't mean anything.

She went back up to seventy. The car with the red paint on its fender did not fall behind.

She told herself to forget the following car and was stern with herself. You have got to imagining things, she told herself. A mind is empty with only the routine of driving to fill it and on a turnpike there is little about driving to occupy the mind. The mind fills itself with trivia, with meaningless concerns. "Don't brood about things," Dr. Strom had told her. "Start your mind going another way."

It was only because the car was so easily identified that she had begun to wonder about it. If there had been no splashes of red paint on one of its front fenders it would have been only a big black car, any big black car, going the way she was going at the speed she was going. I've had bad weeks and the cold has run me down. I am imagining things. I will turn my mind another way—a pleasant, harmless way. I will—I will remember poetry. I will remember Robert Graves's poem about the feline race.

She began to remember Graves aloud for Toby's benefit. Toby liked to hear her voice; he liked her voice cadences. She read from her mind to her cat. She could not remember all of it. She turned the pages of her mind to Yeats. She turned to Frost's "Stopping by Woods on a Snowy Evening."

Poetry had never meant anything to Ben. After the first few months, when what they would do with their evenings was not open to serious question, they had watched television, not read poetry. Or played records, mostly of show tunes. We never talked much, she thought. How long ago was it when I decided it wasn't really very good?

You are brooding again, she told herself. Remember other things about Ben. All right—remember Ben in bed. It was fine in bed.

But one cannot entirely control the memories which seep into a mind emptied by driving a wide and open turnpike. I should not have driven this way alone, she thought.

I should have flown down to Vero. I could have taken Toby with me in his box. But he gets frantic in his box. And I get almost frantic boxed into an airplane. This is all right, and the sun is shining, and tomorrow, or at any rate the next day, I can drive with windows open.

No, don't think of windows. Of the scream fading down from an open window. And, long before that, from a cat on a window ledge ten floors above the ground and a window closed on him. The same window; the kitchen window. But it was an accident. Ben had not seen Toby when he closed the window with Toby outside on the ledge. He had been as concerned as she when Toby had screamed at them from the ledge. Because he knew she was afraid of heights, he had opened the window and started to reach out for the frightened cat. But she had said, "No. No, Ben," and herself reached out for her cat, because Toby was afraid of Ben—a little afraid. (Toby had solved that one; with the window open, Toby had taken his safety into his own paws with one long leap to the center of the kitchen.)

Ben had not seen Toby on the ledge when he closed the window. He had not put Toby on the ledge and closed the window on him. Of course he had not done that. And the car behind is merely a car going south, as I am going south, and going at the speed I am going, which is the speed almost everyone holds to on the turnpike.

She did not look in the rearview mirror. She looked ahead at the wide road.

"Reduce Speed. Toll Booths Ahead."

The Jersey Turnpike widened at its end. She chose her lane to a green light; stopped behind a car from Michigan; moved forward as it moved; held out ticket and money to the attendant; put change in her purse and drove on, more slowly as traffic thickened. She dropped two quarters into a bin and a light turned green in front of her, and she drove, on the inside lane now because trucks lumbered up the slow lane, across the Delaware Memorial Bridge.

Beyond it there was plenty in driving to fill the mind, push memories out of it. She turned left on U.S. 40 and U.S. 13

and edged to the right with slow caution. Along here somewhere, if Maude had remembered rightly, there would be a
Stetson Motel at which she could reserve for the night. And
a restaurant. It was a little after one; it was time for a restaurant. She went very slowly, again behind trucks. "Next
Stetson Lodge, 1 Mile."

There was the replica of a big western hat on top of a
steel pole. The hat was edged with electric lights, which
blinked in spite of sunshine. "Stetson Lodge, Entrance."
She turned in and parked near a sign which said "Office," and
Toby, who had screamed when the car had started far back
in Manhattan, screamed because it had stopped.

Which road was she taking south? Yes, the traffic was
much lighter on three-oh-one. There was a Stetson at—yes,
at Waldorf. Oh, about a hundred and fifty miles. A single
room and bath? But all the rooms had baths. "We *welcome*
pets."

The pleasant woman behind the counter turned away
from it to a machine and pushed buttons on the machine.
The machine rasped. It also clicked. It produced a slip of
paper with a good deal of printing on it and "O.K." in rather
faded type. Carol produced her credit card and it was run
through another machine. She signed her name. A restaurant?

It was right over there. She circled the Buick right over
there and parked where the car was in the sun. It was not
a hot sun. She ran the rear windows partly down; she twisted
open a jar of junior beef and spooned it into Toby's pan.
Toby dropped to the floor and smelled his lunch and looked
up at her with his What-are-you-trying-to-do-to-me? expression. He also said, "Yow-ow." He had lived on junior beef,
with cereal pellets added, since he was a kitten. Carol, who
liked junior beef too, licked the spoon.

"Eat your lunch, cat," she told her cat and walked through
crisp air to her own. Seated by a window which gave her a
complete view of a road full of trucks, she thought, If you
drink don't drive, and ordered a martini, very dry with a
twist. It was dry, it had a twist, it was not especially potent.
But the toast of her club sandwich was crisp toast, and

the coffee was strong and hot. She did not hurry over lunch; she had a cigarette with her second cup of coffee. It seemed a little warmer when she went out to the car, and Toby, in spite of what he had told her about his lunch, had eaten it. He had curled up in the back seat and gone to sleep.

There had been perhaps twenty cars parked in the restaurant's lot when she went in for lunch. Now there were only half a dozen. And none of them had splotches of red on its right front fender.

She almost laughed at her own relief. There had never been anything to be concerned about. The marked car had merely been going about its own business, which happened to coincide with hers.

She ran the car windows up from the control panel at her side, leaving her own window a little open. She edged out into traffic and again was hemmed by trucks. Here, in New Castle, Delaware, the roadway with its several numbers was six lanes wide. When a chance came—it was becoming easier now to alert herself to chances—she inched left to faster lanes. She must watch now. Somewhere along here the road she wanted branched to the left.

Ahead there was a steel trestle across the road with signs on it. "Rts. 13 & 301, Keep Left." "Route 40, Keep Right." She edged over another lane, watching side mirror, rear mirror. And in the rear mirror was the big car with red on its fender.

She got her chance and made it into the extreme left lane. The car with the blotched fender did not follow her into it, although there was, momentarily, room enough for it to wedge in behind her. It stayed to the right, in the lane next to the main truck lane.

The car ahead of her showed its stop lights and, ahead, she could see traffic lights turn red. She slowed; stopped when the car ahead of her stopped.

The car with the daubed fender did not stop, nor did any of the traffic to her right. That traffic, the car with the fender locked in it, bore to the right while she waited for the traffic lights to change. Of course—on Route 40, bound for Baltimore, or toward Baltimore.

The lights released her part of the Y-split traffic, and she moved with the traffic. To her own surprise, she took a deep breath—a breath of relief. "Don't imagine things." Dr. Strom had told her that.

I'm dragged down by all that has happened, she told herself. My mind is still shaky from the shock; bemused still because of this dragging cold. I have been inventing things to worry about; raking my mind for anxieties.

# 4

After a few miles of relatively open driving on a divided highway, she turned where a sign pointed: "U.S. 301," and a smaller sign under it, with an arrow bending in the same direction, said, "Bay Bridge." She went to her right, onto a road which was sometimes narrow and sometimes wide; which twisted and joined other roads and left them and remained 301. She crossed a high, narrow bridge and, far below, sunlight sparkled on water. Three-oh-one became 50 and bypassed Annapolis. 301 had a sign and an arrow, and she twisted off the fast four-lane to the right and was going south again, with the lowering sun in her eyes. She snapped down the sun shield and went south through Maryland.

She had to switch on her lights before a sign told her, "Next Stetson Lodge, 3 Miles." Three minutes or so later a sign said, "Stetson Lodge, Waldorf. Entrance." She turned into a wide drive and circled a swimming pool drained for the winter, but with deck chairs emptily around it. An electric sign said, "Office," and she stopped there and inside pushed her reservation slip across the counter.

Would she like to be near the restaurant? Then—let's see, now. Room 7. That was near the restaurant, but not too near. The young woman behind the counter tapped a bell, and a boy came out from somewhere. "Room Seven for Mrs. Sanders, Bobby," the young woman said, and Bobby said, "This way, ma'am," and went out of the office. Carol followed him and got into her car and crept after him as Bobby, a gangling boy but a brisk walker, went along the low, crescent-shaped building. After what seemed a considerable distance, Bobby stopped and began, with both hands, to beckon her in.

White lines made a slot with "7" painted on the pavement. She crept into it; stopped when Bobby held up both hands, palms toward her. She got out of the car and walked toward the back of it, sorting out her trunk key. And, walking the few steps, she found that she was stiff and tired. Bobby joined her. Bobby said, "Help you, Mrs. Sanders?" and she found she was glad of help. She opened the trunk and pointed to the two bags, among many bags, she wanted. She snapped Toby's leash from its hook; carried her cat and his food and toilet pans. Bobby opened a door marked "7" and she went into a big warm room, thickly carpeted and containing two double beds. Bobby turned on the lights. Carol said, "I wanted a single," and Bobby said, "They're all the same, ma'am," and put her bags on a low bench at the end of one of the beds. He said, "Get you some ice, ma'am," not as a question, and went out of the room, closing the door after him.

Carol sat in a low chair and stretched her legs out. It was fine not to have her feet constrained by floor boards, placed by gas and brake pedals. Toby, who had slept, or at any rate, not talked, all afternoon, curled in her lap and continued to catch up on his sleep. Carol said, "Come in," in answer to a knock, and Bobby came in with an ice container and put it on a desk which was also a chest of drawers and said, "That's a fine cat, ma'am. Siamese, ain't he?" Toby waked up and looked at Bobby and said, "Yow-oh," but was restrained about it.

Carol said, "Yes, he's a Siamese," and reached into the handbag in the chair beside her and fished a quarter out of it and got, "Thank you, ma'am," as if it had been a dollar. She also got, "When you go out, ma'am, you just press the little button in the knob. That locks it." She said, "I'll remember."

Bobby went out of Room 7 and closed the door, tenderly, behind him. Carol unbuckled Toby's harness, and he looked around at her in surprise. Then he jumped off her lap, as if he had suddenly remembered something, and began to smell his way around the room. He went under both the wide beds and came out from under them and went to a closed door at the end of the room and looked up at it and turned and looked at Carol. He said, "Yow-uh?"

"Probably, cat," Carol said and got out of the chair, feeling she creaked a little, and opened the door for Toby. It opened, as Toby apparently had guessed, on a bathroom. She said, "All right, cat," and carried his toilet pan into the bathroom and put it on the floor. Toby smelled the cat litter which half filled it and walked back into the carpeted room and sat in front of Carol and looked up at her and said, "Ow?"

Again she said, "All right, cat," and again got up and opened one of the two flat cases and took a jar of junior beef and a spoon out of it. It was the utility bag, and there was a variety of things in it, including a bottle which was labeled, "House of Lords Gin. Imported," but which actually held four-fifths of gin and one of dry vermouth. ("You'll find some of the states are *dry*, dear," Maude had written in one of the several letters which had urged Carol to get out of that *awful* climate.)

Carol fed her cat, who didn't want to eat at the moment. She left the utility case open. She thought, I might as well. It's been a long day. She found glasses in the bathroom, stiffly sealed in plastic, and prized one out of its hygienic wrapping and put ice in it and poured mixed martini on the ice. She turned back the spread on one of the beds and took off her shoes and stretched on the bed. It was wonderful to stretch legs, to be away from trucks. She lighted a cigarette and sipped, and made her small drink, and the relaxation it slowly brought, last for half an hour. The first day on the road is always the hardest day, Carol Sanders thought. Nerves tighten on the first day and anxiety churns in the mind. How ridiculous I was about that car. Before

( 49 )

I get to Vero, a dozen cars will keep their distance behind me, as this one did. I will not imagine things about them.

Relaxed by the small drink, by the softness of the big bed and the warmth of the room, she grew sleepy, for minutes almost dozed. But she roused herself. Tomorrow would be another long day on the road. She must eat early and get to bed so that she could get up early in the morning. She said, "Sorry, Toby," to the cat who had come to stretch out beside her, and swung out of bed. She wasn't stiff any more; she wasn't tired any more. She coughed experimentally to see if the cold still hung on her, and the cough was not really a cough.

She showered and changed. The room, as she dressed, seemed very warm—seemed much too warm. She found a thermostat and that it was set at eighty and turned it down to seventy. She partly opened one of the two windows at the end of the room, making sure it was screened against the escape of the cat. Chilly air came in through the window; it was still late November, even in southern Maryland. When she went out, remembering to push the button in the knob before she closed the door, remembering to put the key in a big pocket of her loose coat, the air was sharp in her lungs. The air pushed against her, but gently, as she walked under a low overhang past Rooms 6 and 5 and 4 toward the electric sign at the tip of the crescent which said "Restaurant." Above the restaurant sign there was a big western hat, and lights flickered to outline the hat.

The first door she came to was marked "Lounge," and she opened that door and walked into a place of clatter and many voices.

It was a long room with a bar along one side. Along the opposite wall, and again along the rear wall, slot machines stood in ranks. Men and women stood in front of many of the slot machines and poked coins into them and pulled levers down, and the machines whirred and rang bells and, loudly, one of the men who had been pushing coins into a slot said, "Damn it to hell!" He went over to the bar and joined several other men at the bar. He said, still loudly, "I'm jinxed. That's what it is. Jinxed." He wore a checked woolen shirt, but he didn't have on a western hat.

Carol stood just inside the door of the clattering room, and it seemed, for a moment, to shake around her. A woman with a high-pitched voice said, "Wow!" sounding slightly like Toby, and scooped coins out of a cup at the bottom of one of the machines. She clutched the coins and moved to another machine and began, hurriedly, to poke them into it. She yanked the machine's arm down violently after each coin.

I must, Carol thought, be in the wrong place. It said "Restaurant," but this—she saw, at the end of the room, over a door, an electric sign which said "Dining Room." She went down the long room, with the bar on one side and machines chattering on the other, and through the doorway. She went into a quiet room with people—a good many people—sitting quietly at tables. It was about seven, then, but many of the people were having dessert and coffee. A pleasant woman in a gray dress met her just inside the door and said, "One, miss?"

"Yes," Carol said and then, "I guess I came in the wrong way."

"Either way's all right," the pleasant, rather plump woman said. "If you'll come this way, miss."

Carol followed the pleasant woman to a table for two against the wall.

"You mean," she said, when she had sat down on the chair pulled out for her, "anybody can just—walk in? With all those slot machines?"

"Oh," the woman said, "of course, miss. People do ask me that. Out-of-state people. They're perfectly legal in this county, miss. Except on Sundays, of course." She put a menu in front of Carol and smiled at her and said, "Enjoy your dinner," and went away. A girl in a black dress and a white apron, with a white cap perched on the back of improbably red hair, came to the table and said, "A cocktail before dinner, miss?"

Carol ordered a martini, very dry, and suggested House of

Lords. The girl repeated "House of Lords?" with doubt in her voice. "I don't know whether—Beefeater?"

Carol said, "All right," and the girl went away. She came back very quickly with a glass and what appeared to be a very small milk bottle. There was an olive in the empty glass and Carol said, "Wait," as the waitress lifted the little milk bottle, which clearly did not hold milk. She fished the olive out of the glass and nodded and the waitress poured martini into the small cocktail glass. She did not empty the bottle. "Dividend," she said, with pride in her voice. "The roast sirloin is special tonight, miss. With baked Idaho potato. The Maryland fried chicken's good too."

"If I can have the beef rare," Carol said. "After I've finished my drink."

"You just take your time, honey," the waitress said. "French or Thousand Island?"

"Oil and vinegar, please," Carol said and was looked at doubtfully but then nodded at. The waitress went away, and Carol lighted a cigarette and took a sip from her glass, and the waitress came back and put a small wooden bowl partly filled with lettuce, but including also a greenish tomato, in front of her. She put two small cruets down beyond the salad. Carol moved the bowl out of the way and sipped her drink and looked around the room. It was a pleasant room, done in shades of yellow. Even some quite good restaurants nowadays serve salad as a first course, Carol thought. Ben used to make a fuss about it, but it doesn't matter. He made a fuss about a good many things which didn't matter. Of course, when Toby ate part of one of his tennis socks, he did have a point. I suppose that, often, he had a point. I must have loved him. I wish he had told me about that awful sickness. I might, at least, have shared his fear.

She turned her mind away from that and finished the martini in her glass and poured from the tiny container which was shaped so like a milk bottle. The "dividend" half filled the small cocktail glass. It was a good martini, if a little one. Perhaps she would have another, since they were so small. Another and ask for a lemon twist and—

The waitress put a tray down on a stand nearby. She brought a plate to the table, holding it in a napkin. She said, "Nice and rare, miss—you don't like your salad?"

"Later, probably," Carol said. "The meat looks just right."

Suddenly, she was hungry. The roast sirloin, if not especially rare, was good. The baked potato, extricated from its aluminum foil, was dry and flaky. Under the napkin which covered the bread basket there were biscuits and squares of cornbread, instead of hard rolls. Everything was fine.

She lingered over coffee and cigarette. When she went out she went as she had come, and the slot machines still whirred and clattered and there were more men at the bar. Carol went to the door and then turned back. She got a quarter out of her purse and put it in a slot and pulled down an arm.

The machine whirred, and pictures of fruits and bells rotated in front of her. The machine stopped and appeared momentarily to consider. Then it clattered, and she scooped three quarters out of a cup under the rotating symbols. Everything was fine, and outside the moon was full, and now the breeze blew her toward her room and toward sleep, which would be welcome. Everything around was white with moonlight.

When she had gone out to dinner, cars had been thinly scattered in front of doors of the crescent-shaped motel. Now almost all the parking spaces were filled, and lights were on in almost all the rooms. A big black car was in the slot next hers, the slot marked "8." And a Mercedes was in the slot marked "6." This Stetson Lodge had all the business it could conveniently cope with.

She got her key out of the pocket of her loose blue coat and was about to push it into the lock of Room 7 when she remembered. "We always make our reservations in the evening for the next night," Maude had written, instructing the inexperienced. "In the mornings, mostly, there's nobody *around*."

Carol dropped the key backed into her pocket and walked

the curving path to the office. Moonlight reached in under the overhang, and the overhang posts made black shadows across the path. At the office, two couples were at the counter. One of the men pushed a reservation slip across the counter and got a key. But to the other man the clerk, a man this time, said, "Sorry. Full up," and pointed to a little sign on the counter which read "No Vacancy."

The rejected man said, "Any idea where?"

"Maybe Ned's place," the desk clerk said. "Couple miles down the road. Tell you what, I'll give Ned a ring for you."

Carol sat in one of the several chairs in the lobby and lighted a cigarette and waited. The fortunate couple followed the boy, who still was Bobby, out of the office; the defeated were told that Ned could take care of them and went off to be taken care of. The clerk said, "Something I can do for you, miss?" and when told what he could do, said, "About how far, miss? You're going south?"

"Not more than four hundred miles," Carol said. "Yes, I'm going south." She added, "To Vero Beach," not that her destination was of interest to anybody but herself.

There were many details, and details take time. It was fifteen minutes before Carol walked back to Room 7 with a reservation slip for a Stetson Lodge in Wilmington, North Carolina, in her handbag. The breeze was against her again, and it was colder. It would be good to get into the warmth of her room. Only, with a window open and the thermostat turned down, it probably wouldn't be really warm. To get under the warmth of blankets, to stretch out and sleep. That would be fine.

The room was cool when she went into it. But the air was stale with the odor of smoked cigarettes. She switched on lights and said, "Toby?" and looked around. Toby was not stretched on the bed, as she had left him. He had, predictably, gone under something to hide when he heard her key in the lock. She repeated his name, more loudly. She got no answer.

It's odd the room didn't air out, she thought, and called "Toby? Toby!" I left one of the windows open. Still speaking her cat's name, she walked the length of the room. The window she was sure she had left open—the window she had made certain was screened against Toby's escape— was closed. A night maid had closed it? But there was nothing to indicate there had been a night maid. The beds had not been opened; the thrown-back spread of the one she had dozed on was as she had left it.

"Toby," she said, more loudly. "Here, Toby."

No tawny cat with brown ears and mask, brown stockings and tail, came out of anywhere. Toby had done his disappearing act. It was one of his favorite acts. It amused him to be looked for. At hiding, Toby was most devious. He could, when he wanted to, vanish in an unfurnished room, one without hiding places.

Of course, for hiding, beds came first. Carol lay on the floor and looked under the bed she had lain on. She could see through under the other bed. But she could not see her cat. She kept on calling him and he did not answer, and he was an answering cat.

Not under either of the chairs. There was hardly room under the chest. But cats, intent on hiding, can get into places where there is, evidently, no room for them. He was not under the chest. He was not in the bathroom. "Toby. *Toby-cat.*"

Of course. The closet where she had hung the clothes she changed from. The closet had sliding doors and they were closed. But Toby was quite capable of going into a closet and tugging sliding doors to behind him.

She went to the closet quickly, because now anxiety was beginning to grow again. She pulled one of the doors open and tugged down on a light cord.

Toby was not in the closet. She continued to call her cat's name even after she realized that Toby was not anywhere in Room 7, not crouched anywhere, under anything, waiting to be found. Screened window and locked door— these were beyond even Toby.

*Somebody has let Toby out,* she thought, the thought loud and quivering in her mind. *Somebody's stolen him.*

She went to the window she had left open and pulled it open again. She leaned out of it and thought suddenly,

( 55 )

Why, I *can* lean out of it. But there was a screen. I know there was a screen.

She looked down. There was a screen. It was not in the window. It was propped, below the window, against the side of the building. She saw, then, the outside loop-screws to which it had been hooked.

She called her cat's name out of the open window; she called it, loudly, to right and left.

The areaway behind the motel was paved; ten feet or so from the window there was a brick wall, which followed the curved contour of the building as far as she could see in either direction. It was not a high wall; it was something Toby could have gone to the top of in an easy leap. And leaped down from, on the other side, as easily.

Somebody had unhooked the screen and—and gone into her room through the window? Grabbed Toby and gone out of the window with him? Having thought he was a valuable cat?

But he isn't, she thought. He's not a breeding cat, and only breeding cats are really worth money. Whoever stole my cat didn't know that. Just knew, thought he knew, that purebred cats are worth—

She did not finish the thought. She sat on the window sill and swung her legs over and dropped to the pavement outside. She walked along the corridor the building and the wall behind it made and called the name of her cat. She walked past lights in windows and heard music and words from television sets come through them. A man appeared at one of the windows and looked at her. She said, "Have you seen a cat? A Siamese cat?"

The man said, "Nope, lady. Sorry," and closed the window. The window he had stood behind was screened; all the other windows she had walked past were screened. She kept on calling Toby's name and walking the passage between wall and building. She had taken her coat off in the room while she looked for Toby, and cold air wrapped her and crept into her. "Toby! *Toby?*"

She was walking toward the office, in the center of the crescent. She came to a blocking wall. There was a door in the wall, but it was locked when she tried to open it. She walked back the way she had come, still calling the name of her cat—looking ahead for him in the moonlight, looking up at the top of the wall she walked beside. She went past her open window and to the other, nearer, end of the passageway. She came to another locked door in a transverse wall.

She walked back to her open window and pushed the screen out of her way and climbed back into the window. She would go out and look and call in front of the curved building. Toby could have, somehow, got on that side. He might be out there in the moonlight, hiding under a car. Or —run over by one of the cars which had come in while she was at the restaurant? Cats cannot gauge the speed of moving cars. Toby—

Toby was sitting in the middle of the room, washing his face with his right forepaw. He said, "Yah-ah-aw!" loudly, in a tone of indignation.

"*You!*" Carol said, as indignantly as her cat. "Were you here all the time?"

Toby jumped up on one of the beds. He said merely "Myah," which might have meant anything.

It's possible he was here all the time, Carol thought. I suppose it's possible.

But she did not really think it possible. She had looked too thoroughly and too long. Toby had gone out through an open window, and he had come back the same way. And somebody had taken the screen out of the window so that he could. Then, somehow, enticed him out? And then closed the window, from outside, after him?

Carol went back and closed the window she had left open and pulled curtains over it. She sat down in one of the chairs and lighted a cigarette. Toby curled up on the bed and went partly to sleep, but kept slanting eyes a little open.

I'm too jittery to go to sleep, Carol thought. She walked across the room to the big television set. A card taped with a message typed on it. "Channels 5, 8 and 10 only. Cable Television."

She switched on Channel 5 and got the middle of a movie;

she turned to 8 and got a girl in tights, singing with her head raised and her eyes half closed. A good many men and women were dancing behind her. She tried Channel 10 and got a woman scrubbing a sink with a new and improved cleaning powder. She switched the television off, since nothing on it seemed likely to lessen her jitters, and went back to her chair and lighted another cigarette.

Toby, forgiving her for her desertion, came over and sat on her lap and purred. She put her free hand on his smooth warm coat, and the jitters diminished. After half an hour or so, and several more cigarettes—too many more, she thought—she undressed and turned out lights and got into bed.

Somebody deliberately let him out, she thought, waiting for sleep. Did that to—to disturb me. Unless—

Another thought came into her mind, at first dimly and then with greater brightness.

It's the time of year, she thought, when people take down screens for the winter. Mine was the only screen I saw that had been taken down, but a man who takes down screens must start somewhere. You'd think he'd start at one end or the other, not here, which is more or less in the middle. But people have their own ways of doing things.

That's what it was; that's almost certainly what it was. Just somebody starting to take down the screens for the winter. Not knowing—and why should he know—? that I had my cat in here and that cats like to jump through open windows? And, because it was no longer screened, closing the window?

Slowly, then, she slipped into sleep. The jangle of a bell yanked her out of it. The ringing seemed very close; it seemed to grow louder as she wakened. It was a telephone bell.

In the darkness she groped for the bedside lamp and her fingers found it, but for what seemed like a long time, while the telephone went on jangling, she could not in the darkness find a way to turn the light on. Then her groping fingers found a knob in the base of the lamp and twisted it, and then it was light in the room. The telephone still rang. She found it on a shelf under the bedside table and lifted the receiver and said "Hello?"

A man answered her. He said, "Molly? Hope I didn't wake you up."

She said, "Who do you want?" Her voice was still husky with sleep and her mind foggy with it. Then she said, "Molly?"

"Wake up, girl," the man said. "You sound as if you don't know who you are."

"I'm not Molly," Carol said. "You've got the wrong number."

"Room you told me," the man said. "You aren't Molly Drayton?"

"No," she said, and she could hear her voice shaking. The hand which held the receiver shook with her voice, and the receiver trembled against her ear.

"Sure I had it right," the man said. "Sure she said Room Seven. Hope I didn't wake you up, miss—"

She thought he waited to be told her name. "It's all right," she said.

"I'm sure sorry," the man said. "Sorry as hell I waked you up."

She said again, meaninglessly, that it was all right and heard the click as he hung up. For some seconds she did not put her own receiver back in its cradle. She held it out before her and watched the hand which held it shake. Then, slowly, feeling the movement uncertain, the task incredibly complicated, she put the receiver back in its stand.

And one thought revolved in her mind; seemed to ring there as the bell had rung.

It was Ben's voice, Carol thought. *Ben's voice.* But Ben is dead. Somewhere, a long time ago, Ben fell out of a window and was killed. But this was Ben's voice. Ben's. Ben's!

I'm going out of my mind, Carol thought. Dr. Strom said I would be all right, but I'm not all right. It couldn't have been Ben, because Ben is dead. Things seem to be what they can't be, and that means I'm going out of my mind. This man didn't say "Drayton." He said something that sounded like it. "Creighton." That must have been it. Or "Layton." Perhaps it was Layton.

Because before Ben and I were married my name was Drayton. Carol Drayton. Not Molly. Carol. *Carol.*

She got out of bed, slowly and carefully. She went into the bathroom. Toby was curled on the other bed. He was asleep. But always telephone bells wakened him, and always he went to telephones to help answer them.

But I know the telephone rang and that I answered it, and that it was Ben's voice. It wasn't a nightmare—a hallucination. Because now I am awake and on my feet and looking at myself in the mirror and I am Carol Sanders, who was once Carol Drayton. I have brown hair.

She reached up and touched her hair. She pushed it back because it had fallen over her eyes.

I have blue eyes. They are as blue as Toby's eyes. I am Carol Sanders. I am awake. Anybody can imagine things; voices can sound like other voices. A man may start anywhere when he is taking down screens. Cars on highways always are behind other cars.

She splashed cold water on her face. She toweled off and looked again at it in the mirror.

Ben said, "Your lovely face," Carol thought. It's an all-right face. In its way it's a pretty face. It's Carol Sanders's face. It's—it couldn't have been Ben on the telephone. I was half asleep. Perhaps I had been dreaming about Ben, although I do not remember a dream about him. I—

She walked back into the bedroom. Toby was sitting up on the bed now and looking at her. She went back to her own bed and took the telephone off its shelf and lifted the receiver and put it to her ear. Her hand wasn't shaking as much as it had been.

The telephone hummed faintly at her, but nothing else happened. She got the stand off the shelf and looked at the dial, and one hole in it was marked "Office." She put a finger in that hole and spun the dial, and the telephone made a different sound. After almost a minute a voice said, "Office. Can I help you?"

The voice, she thought, was a boy's voice. She said, "Is this Bobby?"

"Yes'm."

"This is Mrs. Sanders, in Room Seven."

"Yes, Miz Sanders. I know which room it is."

"You—somebody—just put a call through to this room," she said. "A—a man who wanted somebody else."

Bobby said, "I'm sorry about that, Miz Sanders."

"Was it somebody in the motel? Or was it a call from outside?"

"Outside, ma'am. Could have been from anywhere, I guess."

"Did this man ask for me by name? Or did he just say, 'Room Seven, please'? Something like that?"

"Just the room number, ma'am. Like you said. 'Room Seven, please.' "

She said, "It waked me up, Bobby. It wasn't your fault, of course, but it waked me up. Will you do this, Bobby? Not put any more calls through tonight?"

"Sure, Miz Sanders. I sure won't. Anyway, we shut the switchboard down at ten o'clock, and it's pretty near that now."

She said, "All right, Bobby. Good night."

Bobby said, "Good night, Miz Sanders. Sorry you got waked up."

My voice didn't shake when I talked to him, Carol thought. I was perfectly coherent when I talked to him.

She went to the utility bag and opened it and got out of it a little bottle with a prescription number and instructions typed on a label. "One or two at bedtime for sleep," she read, and shook two capsules out of the almost-full bottle. She carried them into the bathroom and ran water into a glass and swallowed the two capsules. She went back to bed and waited.

Toby had curled into sleep again. Toby didn't need capsules to make him sleep.

# 5 ✑

She wakened because Toby was standing on her and saying anxious things to her. She tried to push him away and thought, dimly, that he should not be there. He was not allowed in her bedroom at night; the rest of the apartment was his to roam in or to sleep in. She said, dimly, "Go away, cat." He did not go away. He repeated, more loudly, what he had said before.

She really wakened then, thought: Toby and I are in a motel room. We are going—

The thought drifted away in a kind of haze. What replaced it was not a thought but a feeling of apprehension. It was formless, had no center. It was a feeling she had not known since—since she was going once a week to Dr. Strom. But he promised me—

It's because of those sleeping pills, she told herself. I'm not used to them. On the prescription label it says, "One or two," but I've never taken two before. Why did I take two last night? I am groggy because I took two capsules. I took them because—

She sat up in bed. Toby jumped off the bed and sat beside it and made remarks up to her.

Because, she thought, somebody telephoned and got the wrong number and waked me up. And because I was half asleep when I answered I thought his voice was like Ben's voice. And—oh, yes—because yesterday I had the crazy notion that a car was following me. And because I thought, absurdly thought, that somebody had deliberately let Toby out of this room to—to trouble me. I must have been very tired yesterday to imagine such things. The first day of a long drive is a tiring day, an upsetting day.

She swung out of bed, and the grogginess, the vague apprehension began to seep out of her mind. She went to the bathroom and Toby followed her, yammering. His plate was empty. That was why he had wakened her by standing on her and talking to her anxiously. She said, "All right, Toby," and turned the hot water on in the basin and let it run while she got his jar of junior beef from the utility case and spooned food into his pan. He began to eat, his tongue making a scraping sound on the metal.

She dipped instant coffee into one of the glasses. The water from the basin faucet was hot, or almost hot. She let it run a little longer, but it did not get hotter. When she had showered the night before, the water had been scalding. Probably it is too early in the morning for it to be really hot.

She looked at her watch. It was not really early. It was eight-thirty. She had meant to be on the road by eight-thirty; miles on the road by eight-thirty. "Three hundred and fifty miles. Perhaps a little more." It would be after dark, long after dark, when she turned in at the Stetson Lodge in Wilmington, North Carolina. But her room would be waiting for her. She had a little slip which promised that.

She ran the now hot-enough water into the powdered coffee and carried the glass back to her bed and got back into the bed and drank the coffee and smoked a cigarette. She told herself, I must get going. I *must* get going. But for some minutes she did not get going. For those minutes the tasks of getting out of bed and dressing and walking to the restaurant seemed insurmountable tasks. It's those pills, she thought. I shouldn't have taken those pills. Even with them, something waked me up last night.

She had not, until that moment, remembered that she had been wakened in the night after she had taken the sleeping pills. Wakened—wakened because somebody had turned the lights on? That was it; light had wakened her. Somebody had come into the room and turned the lights on. No, that isn't right. The light—

There wasn't any light, she thought. I dreamed there was a light. I dreamed the light waked me up. She thought, Snap out of it. *Snap out of it.*

She got out of bed quickly and dressed hurriedly. She put the things she had used from her bags back into them and put Toby's harness on, in spite of his squirming, and hitched him to a chair leg. "No more wandering for you, cat," she told Toby, who said, "Yah-*ow*" rather loudly. She made sure the window she had climbed out of and back through was closed and realized she had left it closed all night, and had not opened the other window, which still was screened. Whoever took the screens down for winter at the motel hadn't gone on with it. Other things to do in the morning, probably. Or he had gone back to the work of descreening somewhere else.

It was bright outside and the air was crisp. She breathed deeply of the crisp air and it seemed to blow through her mind, blowing apprehension out of it.

The door marked "Lounge" was locked, and she went around the restaurant to the main door. There were not many having breakfast in the restaurant. She was late for breakfast. But coffee came at once and orange juice with it, and she had just finished the juice when toast and soft-boiled eggs came, the waitress trotting with them.

She ate quickly, said, "No, thank you," to the offer of more coffee; was suddenly in a hurry to be on her way; to be driving south toward warmth. Maude says that the houses —hers and her brother's and Ben's, which now is mine— are almost on the beach and that it is, because it is quite a way down something called Ocean Drive, almost a private beach. I'll sit on the beach in sunshine and bake the remnants of this cold out of me.

She carried her light bags to the car and put them in the trunk. She carried Toby out and hooked him to his eye screw and went back once more for his toilet pan and his dinner pan. A lithe ten-pound cat, who doesn't want to go anywhere in a car, is of himself enough to carry.

She got behind the wheel of the eager little Buick and strapped herself there and pushed the ignition key into its lock and turned it.

And all that happened was a discouraged click from under the hood.

Cold. But, no. The coldness has nothing to do with the starter. The starter burrs at command, whatever the temperature. The engine may be obdurate, although this engine had never been. But the starter—

She turned the key back and made sure that the gear selector pointed to "P" for "park." She pumped on the gas pedal and tried again. This time she got a "clug" instead of the distant click. She pumped again.

It can't be the battery, she thought. They checked everything before I started, and they have always been thorough. And all day yesterday I drove, with the lights off most of the time, and all day the battery was charging, if it needed to charge. It *can't* be dead.

She pumped on the gas pedal. If the starter ever turned the engine over, it would need all the help it could get. She pumped until she began, through the partly open window, to smell gasoline. If I've flooded it—

She turned the key again, wishing she believed—really believed—in something to pray to. There was again a "clug" from under the hood. Then, in a dispirited way, the starter began to whir at her. Each whir seemed to tire it. There was nothing to do but wait, with foot on gas pedal.

The motor coughed, clearing its throat. Then, suddenly, it was roaring. She relaxed her foot on the gas pedal but let the engine run on, still above idling speed. After several minutes she put the lever into reverse and backed out of the parking space. When, at the juncture of the motel's drive and U.S. 301, she stopped to wait a space to fit into on the highway, she raced the motor. The motor roared obedience.

She waited for what seemed a long time for a place in

the traffic of Route 301. A public telephone booth at the juncture of drive and highway partially blocked her view of the road. She edged a little forward until she could see around the booth. When the road was clear she spurted into it and went south through Maryland. Highway driving was familiar now, not insecure as it had been the day before.

She drove across a high bridge into Virginia. A sign said, "Two Way Traffic Ahead," and the road narrowed, and she curbed the eager little car. Driving was no longer a sitting behind a wheel, waiting for miles of pavement to go back under a car. Driving was a matter of keeping a watchful eye on the car ahead and, where traffic bunched, through it to the car beyond; of keeping a watchful eye on cars behind. Driving was a matter, now, of watching for a chance to pass trucks as they slowed on hills—of edging to the left to see around them, of judging the nearness and the speed of approaching cars; of making sure that they were approaching, not in her lane for their own passing.

After fifty miles or so she pulled into a service station, although her gauge still showed a quarter of a tank. A tall blond young man came to her and said, "Fill her up, miss?" She said, "Please. With high test. And will you check under the hood?" He said, "Sure will, miss," and plugged the pump hose into the car. He washed the windshield; he washed the rear window and rubbed a cloth over the side mirror. He raised the hood and checked the oil and pushed the measuring rod back into it; he unscrewed the cap of the radiator and looked into that and put the cap on again. He unscrewed plugs on the battery and looked into the battery and screwed the plugs in again.

"Will you check the battery connections?" she asked him and he said, "Sure will, miss," and wiggled terminal connections. He said, "A-O.K., miss," and put the hood down. When he was opposite her window on his way to remove the gas hose she said, "You're quite sure the battery's all right? Doesn't need water or whatever they need."

He said it sure looked O.K.

"Because when I tried to start this morning," Carol said,

"it seemed to be dead, but then it was all right."

"Plenty of water in the cells," the blond man said. "I'll check it if you want me to, but—"

The gas pump quit whirring. He went back and jiggled the lever on the hose and the pump whirred briefly and stopped. He came back to her window and said, "Five ninety even, miss. Check the battery if you want me to."

She paid him. He said, "Better see if she starts all right now."

She twisted the ignition key and the starter whirred and the motor caught.

"Sounds fine now," the blond man said. "Didn't forget to switch your lights off last night, did you, miss? Leave lights on and they pull the battery down, you know."

She had put her lights on before she got to the motel. But she was certain she had turned them off. She had passed the car, pointed at her room, as she walked to the restaurant and would have walked into the glare of its lights if they had been glaring. She was certain the lights had not been glaring. She was certain the lights had been off.

But what she said was, "Oh, I'm sure I did. I always do."

Which was less than certainty.

"Anyhow, it's O.K. now," the man said. "Come back and see us again, miss."

She edged again into the traffic of 301. "Divided Highway Ahead." "Divided Highway Ends. Two Way Traffic Ahead."

For miles as she neared Richmond, Route 301 went, narrowly, up hills and down hills. For half an hour an Army convoy of many trucks went up and down hills, slowly, ahead of her. She crept behind it, the trucks too close together to pass among them. And behind her, behind the convoy, a long slow tail of cars crept. An adventurer pulled out to go around her; pulled back in again. And northbound cars went gayly past, seeming exultant in their freedom.

Finally, a sign said, again, "Divided Highway Ahead." The adventurer, taking his chances—and hers with them—shot around her. She signaled and was next and had cleared the creeping convoy before a sign warned that the divided highway ended and that ahead there was two-way traffic.

It was almost noon when 301 became also Interstate 95 and then Route 1 and then, "Richmond-Petersburg Turnpike." She went around Richmond in a surge of cars, all moving very fast. Cars and trucks left the turnpike at signs which gave exit numbers and said, "To Downtown Richmond." Cars came onto the turnpike. "Merging Traffic." She dropped quarters into bins and lights turned from red to green. A sign said "U.S. 1," and the arrow pointed to the right. A sign said, "U.S. 301," and the arrow pointed toward the sky.

She paid a final toll. A sign said, "Interstate 95 Ends." But the road did not end; it became "301 South." It was divided and filled with cars and trucks, but there was room for all of them. "Business 301." "Bypass 301." "Through Traffic Keep Right." She was through traffic; she kept right.

"Just beyond one of the good Howard Johnsons you go left," Maude had written her. "I've forgotten the route number, but I think the sign says 'To Goldsboro.' Or perhaps it's 'Greensboro.' Anyway, it takes you to Wilmington and Route 17, if that's the way you decide to go. Bill and I always cut across there and, if we've got an early enough start, have lunch at that Howard Johnson's. It's the one on the right."

Carol had worked it out on her map and drawn a blue line along the route she was to follow. When she stopped for lunch—which she began to realize would be a good deal short of the recommended Howard Johnson's before the turnoff—she would check on her map.

Meanwhile—meanwhile, Emporia (which she had always thought was somewhere out west, probably in Kansas) and a restaurant which looked possible and had a sign in front which read, "Come As You Are."

She pulled in there and parked with other cars. Toby, who had slept the morning away, curled on the back seat— with only occasional intervals of standing on hind feet and looking out of windows—yelled hunger. She fed him, ran windows down so that there were cracks for air, but not enough for cats. She pressed down a plunger to lock the door on her right, and, vaguely, wondered why she did this. She did not usually lock the door of the car when she parked it. She had not, she thought, even locked it the night before. Luggage was safe in the trunk. Oh—now so that nobody would have a chance to steal Toby. Not that anyone had, but still—

She had got out of the car, making sure she had her keys to it, and was about to lock the driver's door when she remembered the map on which she had traced her course. She got back in and opened the glove compartment, in which she never carried gloves. The map was in—

The map was not in the glove compartment. There was an envelope marked, "Quick Claim," which was from her insurance company. There was a nest of plastic cups. There was a box of tissues. There was a small can of touch-up paint which matched the paint of the little Buick. There was no map.

But when, in the apartment, Frank had called up to tell her they had brought the car around, and then come up to help her with her bags, she had picked the map up and carried it down in her hand. In the hand which held the handbag. She could see it in her hand as she looked into the glove compartment and could not find the marked map. She had put it in there, and snapped it in, while Frank was stowing luggage in the trunk. She could feel herself putting the map into the compartment. She had had to bang the compartment lid twice to make it catch. She could hear the sound of the banging.

Little puzzles. Little niggling things. It was as if somebody were nibbling at her journey. I'm sure I put the map there, she told herself—told herself with insistence, as if she were trying to convince herself. I am sure I didn't leave the lights on last night. But yesterday I was sure that a car was following me—a car with splotches of red on its right fender. But the car turned off, went toward Baltimore.

She got out of the Buick and knew she had put the car keys safely in her purse, but stood by the car with the door open and checked in her purse. The keys were in it. She had known the keys would be in it. She pressed the button in the door handle and closed the door and tested and found it locked. Then she put her fingers on the latch of her hand-bag because she wanted to open it once more to make sure the keys were there.

She was sharp with herself then. You just made sure the keys were in your handbag, she told herself. Can't you be sure from one minute to the next?

She walked the few feet to the door of the restaurant and opened the door, and a woman who looked rather like the woman of the night before said, "One, miss?" and, when Carol nodded, led her to a table by a window. "Can I get a cocktail?" Carol said, needing one.

"Not in Virginia," the woman said. "We're not allowed to sell by the drink. Except beer and wine, of course. A sherry?"

"Dry," Carol said. "Very dry. Do you have any maps? Virginia? North Carolina?"

"At the cashier's desk," the woman said. "I think maybe. You want the sherry on the rocks, miss?"

Carol did not. She put her opened napkin on the table to mark it as hers and went to the cashier's desk and got a map of North Carolina, with part of Virginia at its top. She went back to the table and found a small glass of sherry waiting for her. She drank the sherry, which after all could have done with ice, and opened the map and found Route 301 and where she was on it. She drank sherry and traced her route south. Just above the North Carolina line, a road branched to the left and she followed it down, slanting south and east across North Carolina. Ending—yes—ending in Wilmington. She got a pencil out of her bag and traced the road.

Did she care to order? She looked up from the map at a black-haired young waitress in a white dress. Or would she like another glass of sherry?

"Yes," Carol said. "And—" She looked at the menu which had luncheon suggestions, all of which looked substantial. She was not hungry. There was a list of sandwiches. "Another glass of sherry, please. And a turkey sandwich."

"Hot, miss?"

"No. Just a turkey sandwich. Without lettuce, please."

The waitress said, "Sherry. And a turkey sandwich. No lettuce. Thank you, miss." The waitress went away. Carol folded the map up, but it did not fold neatly as it had before. She folded the map again, carefully. It seemed important to get it folded as it had been folded before. It should be very easy to fold it as it had been folded before. All she had to do was to crease it where it had been creased before. She gave all her attention to folding the map.

This way. No, the crease is the other way. Then, this way. I must get it right. It is important to get it right.

"Here you are, miss," the waitress said and then, "If you don't mind moving the map, miss."

Carol folded the map up without paying any attention to the way the creases ran. It came out right. It was, for an instant, a kind of meaningless triumph. The waitress picked up the empty sherry glass and put a full one in its place. She said, "Shall I bring your sandwich now, miss? You want coffee with it, miss?"

"Yes."

"Hot coffee, miss?"

They nibble at me, Carol thought. All these trivial things nibble at me. She said, "Please," and the waitress went away.

I dreamed a light wakened me last night, Carol thought. That somebody came into my room and turned the light on. But I had locked the door. Wait a minute. There was a chain on the door and I put it into its slot after Toby was sitting in the middle of the floor washing himself. I closed the window so he could not get out again, and then I made sure the door was locked and put the chain into its slot. I can see myself doing those things, in that order. I'm certain I did these things and did them so—closed the window I had climbed in and then made sure about the door. Did I lock the window? Look back into memory; see yourself doing things last night. Somebody could have come in the window and turned on the light. No. I locked the window.

You're not tracking, she told herself. It is the way it was before. No. I won't have it the way it was before. Dr. Strom told me it wouldn't be. He promised me.

She wrenched at her mind to put it again on a track. She got cigarettes out of her handbag and lighted one, and she sipped her sherry.

The car was pointing at the front window of my room, Carol thought. The car doors were not locked. If somebody had got into the car and turned the lights on they would have shone into the room, because I had only partly closed the Venetian blinds. They stuck a little. And I had not drawn the curtains because, although they looked as if they would, they would not draw. I tried that after the boy named Bobby brought me ice and thanked me for the tip. I did it without thinking, but now I remember doing it. It was before I took Toby's harness off and made myself a drink. I am quite certain that that was the way it was.

Somebody could have got into the car and turned the lights on so they would shine in my window. To wake me up? Why would anybody do that? Or—*of course*. To run the battery down. But why would anybody do that? It doesn't seem to make sense that anybody would do that. Or that somebody would take the screen out of the window so that Toby would go out. Or that somebody would follow me in a car marked so that I would identify it; would know it was following me. But it turned off in Delaware where the roads forked.

Turned the lights on and opened the glove compartment and took the map. But that is meaningless. Maps are given away; there is no reason to steal a map.

Little niggling things, Carol thought. Not meant to harm me. Only meant to—words came into her mind. "He only does it to annoy, because he knows it teases. He only does it to—"

She pushed the words out of her mind, but felt that her mind still jiggled. She was, tried to be, stern with herself. No car followed me. I forgot to turn the lights off when I parked at the motel. Probably I forgot to put the map in the compartment. It was a foggy day, and I am always foggy in the mornings. There is nothing wrong with being foggy in the mornings. It doesn't mean anything.

The waitress put a plate in front of her. The plate had a sandwich, cut diagonally, and potato chips and a slice of greenish tomato. The waitress turned a coffee cup right side up and poured coffee into it from a glass container. She said, "And there you are, miss," and Carol thought, Where am I? and said, "Thank you. It looks very good."

"He only does it to annoy, because he knows—"

The sandwich had lettuce on it. You can always take lettuce out of a sandwich. The sandwich didn't taste of much of anything. They always put lettuce on turkey sandwiches even when you tell them not to. Turkey sandwiches often don't taste of much of anything.

She ate the sandwich and drank the coffee, which was all-right coffee. The waitress said, "Heat it up, miss?" and poured more coffee into the cup. Carol had a cigarette with the coffee and opened the map again, this time carefully, watching the creases, and found the road again—the road that would take her down through North Carolina to a city called Wilmington.

She did not want to go back on the road again, drive many miles again. She wanted to sit here, in the quiet, and smoke cigarettes and drink coffee. I can find a nearer place to stop for the night, she thought. Go on again tomorrow. I am not bound to any time. If I am a day late at Vero I'll be a day late at Vero. It will not make any difference.

She crushed her cigarette out with more force than was needed. She left coins on the table and paid at the cashier's desk and went out to the car. It was warmer in the sun than it had been, and it was good to be warm. She forgot she had locked the car doors and tried to open the one on her side, but then she remembered and got the keys out of her handbag. (I forget things. Perhaps I forgot last night to turn the lights off. I was sure I had not forgotten, but perhaps I did forget. I am sure I was dressing in my room the

( 73 )

day Ben fell and screamed. But I am not sure of anything.)

It was warm in the car, which had been standing in the sun. Toby was not curled on the back seat. He was stretched out on it. When she got into the car he looked up at her through only half-opened eyes. It was unlike Toby not to say anything. Had somebody somehow got into the car and done something to Toby? But I locked the car. "Toby!"

Toby got up and arched his back and said, "Yow-ooow," at considerable length. On the chance he had not been understood, he repeated that, and other things, again at length. He had finished his lunch; he had been having his afternoon nap. He had been disturbed. Sunlight slanted through the rear window of the car and onto the back seat and onto Toby. Anybody, even a human, ought to have been able to see that.

She said, "All right, cat," and put the key into the ignition, and for a moment her fingers would not turn the key. She took a deep breath and made her fingers move, and the motor roared almost instantly. She backed out, circled out, stopped to wait her turn onto Route 301. There was no telephone booth here to block her vision.

She drove south through Virginia, then through North Carolina, on wide roads. "We try to stay off 95," Maude had written her, in careful instruction. "So many people take it that 301 is, part of the time, almost like a country road." Carol tried to stay off Interstate 95. Sometimes 301 joined it for miles and she could not stay off it, but then 301 would branch off again. When it was itself, and only itself, 301 was for the most part four-lane and almost deserted. Filling stations were closed, except where the highway went through towns. Some of them had "For Sale" signs in front of them. So did several motels. But it was a fine, fast road to drive on, if one had a full tank and no need of lodging.

The road was 95 again when it bypassed Wilson. After a time there was a Howard Johnson's on the right, perched on the right. The one Maude had written of? With a left turn toward Wilmington only a mile or so beyond it?

Carol held to the left lane, and trucks, some of them snorting horns at her, passed on the right. "Route 117, Keep Left." "Route 117, Goldsboro. Wilmington," and an arrow hooking toward it. She made her turn. "Two Way Traffic Ahead."

After a time, when there was a space, she pulled off the road and got her map out of the glove compartment. One hundred seventeen. That was right. Her penciled line ran beside it. She pulled back onto the road and went south and east. Traffic was not heavy on this road, but there was enough to driving to fill her mind. With only the routine of driving in it, her mind relaxed. A sign said, "Wilmington, 75 Miles." She had her lights on low by then, to mark her car in traffic. Then she put them up, to show her the way.

It was almost seven when her lights picked up a big sign; "Stetson Lodge, Wilmington, Next Left." Below that were further instructions and she slowed to read them. She was to turn left on U.S. 17. The Stetson Lodge would then be three miles on her right.

She was tired by then, and the car, which had been so warm when she got into it, was cool—cool enough for the heater. And Toby told her from the back seat that it was time for dinner. "Jct. U.S. 17." She crossed an overpass and circled down from it, as signs directed. She came to a wide road full of lights and waited, knowing that she was missing chances. A car behind honked at her with impatience. She saw a chance—not as good as some she had ignored—and took it and was on Route 17, heading south in thickened traffic. And then, ahead and high above the roadway, a western hat twinkled at her. She turned in where the sign said "Entrance" and stopped where another said "Office." For several minutes, then, she merely sat in the car, although she willed herself to get out of it.

Finally she got out of the car, leaving the motor running and the lights on, and went into the office. She pushed her reservation slip across a counter, and the man behind it said, "Yes, ma-am." It's been a long day, she thought. I have aged from "miss."

"New wing all right?" the man said and Carol, with no special idea what he meant, said, "That'll be fine."

"Best rooms we've got," the man said. "This time of evening they're mostly taken. Man had reserved two rooms there, but just now he called in and canceled one of them. Been here before, this man had, I guess. Said just which two rooms he wanted and then decided he didn't want one of them."

Probably, Carol thought, it gets lonely behind a counter when the rush is over. A man behind a counter wants to talk.

"Don't hear the traffic a-*tall* in the wing," the man said, and ran her credit card through its machine. "If you'll just sign here, ma'am." She signed and he tapped a bell, and a boy came through a door behind the counter.

"Room One seventeen for Mrs. Sanders, Roy," the man said and then, to Carol, "He'll show you the way, ma-am."

She was just to follow the arrows. She followed arrows, which took her in a circle of the spreading motel buildings. A flashlight waved and pointed for her; she followed the beam into a slot among cars. "Second floor, ma-am," Roy said. "Help you with the bags, ma-am?" He looked into the back seat. He said, "That a cat, ma-am?" Toby answered for himself.

Carol opened the trunk and pointed at the two bags she wanted. With Toby squirming under one arm and the other hand grasping Toby's pans, Carol followed the boy up a steep flight of concrete stairs and along a balcony and into a big, warm room—a room with two double beds in it, and several tables and a chest and two chairs. And a television set. ("Free Cable Television in Every Room.")

The boy put her cases on stands. He turned on lights until the room glared. He said, "Get you ice, ma-am," and went out and almost immediately came back with an ice container. "Anything else, ma-am?" Roy said.

"A restaurant?"

"Right across the street, ma-am. You just go along back of the lodge and cross the street and there it is. Open till nine-thirty, it is. Best around here."

Carol thanked him; she tipped him. After he had said, "Thank *you*, ma-am," and gone out she took Toby's harness off and found the bathroom and put his pans in it, and food in his eating pan. He walked under her feet as she moved around the room and told her, loudly, to hurry up. She carried a glass back into the room and put ice in it and poured mixed martini on top of the ice and sat in one of the chairs and put her feet up on a stool. After a time—after a time and two cigarettes and a moderate refill of her glass— the stiffness went out of her slim legs.

The TV set stared at her, vacantly, from across the room. She thought, I could turn it on and get the news or something. But I would have to walk across the room to turn it on, and it must be too late for news. I must finish my drink and freshen up and walk behind the lodge and across the street and get myself some dinner. I mustn't forget to eat dinner. I mustn't forget to lock the door before I go out and make sure about the windows.

She looked at her watch. It showed her eight-thirty. Time enough; not all the time in the world, but time enough. She lighted another cigarette. She thought, It's safe here; warm here. Nothing can happen while I sit here. I'm not really hungry enough to walk across a street to a restaurant. I'm too tired to walk behind a building and across a street. I can just—

It is hard to make up my mind to get up and freshen lipstick and brush my hair and walk across a street, she thought, and sipped from her glass and watched Toby come out of the bathroom and look at both the beds and choose his own and jump onto it and turn around three times and curl for sleep. He's a better traveler than I am, she thought. Tomorrow I'll let him drive the car. Now I can just—

The last of the ice in the glass clicked against her teeth. She stubbed her cigarette out and did the things she had to do and went out of the warm room into the cool night and walked along the balcony to the steep stairs. (There ought to be a moon. Last night there was a moon.) She went down the stairs and along a lighted blacktop driveway behind the Stetson Lodge and across a street and up an easy path and into a restaurant. There were not many people in the restaurant, which was softly lighted. The waitresses here wore yellow uniforms. But the Negro girls who carried out trays of used dishes wore white uniforms.

She would not care for a glass of wine with her dinner; yes, she realized they did not serve anything stronger in North Carolina. She looked at the menu. "I'm afraid we're out of the roast beef, ma-am. The swordfish is very good tonight."

The swordfish, when it came, was good. The French fries which came with it were crisp and hot. So, less fortunately to her taste, were the green peas. The bread basket held biscuits and small brown balls. "Hushpuppies, ma-am." They were oniony and sweet and, unexpectedly, good.

Why, Carol thought, eating swordfish and French fries and peas and hushpuppies—why, I'm hungry after all.

She was hungry enough for "homemade" apple pie; relaxed enough to linger over coffee and cigarettes. But she came out of relaxation with guilt when she saw that she was the one customer left in the big room and that the only others eating were six of the waitresses, clustered—and chirpy—at a round table. Because she had, probably, put people to trouble she tipped more than she usually did.

She went out into the cool night and now the moon was out—just coming up and not yet as bright as it had been the night before. But it was a clear moon and no clouds floated across it. And her room was only pleasantly warm when she went back into it, and Toby was curled asleep on his chosen bed and wakened enough to speak to her, but only in welcome.

I was hungry, she thought. Now I am sleepy. Everything is all right now. There aren't any ridiculous fancies now. I'm going toward the South and I will lie on the beach there in the sun, and there will be no more niggling little things.

She went to the window to adjust the Venetian blinds and looked out of it, and down. Somebody—in the parking space next to her now?—had just arrived. His lights were blazing. But she did not see any movement around the lighted car.

Somebody else's lights? Or—*my* lights. I do not remember locking the car doors. I told myself to lock the doors so that what happened—what may have happened—last night would not happen again. But I do not remember locking the car doors.

# 6 ∽

She almost ran across the big room to the closet. I must hurry, she thought. Must hurry, must hurry. The battery will go dead again if I don't hurry.

She put her coat on and went to the door which opened on the balcony. Again, she almost ran to the door. There was a kind of panic in her movements.

She was outside on the balcony and had almost closed the door when she remembered. She must have her key. She must have her key to get back in. She went back into the room and could not remember where she had put the key when she came back after dinner to the room's warmth. The table by the bed? The top of the television set. The—

She found it on the desk and ran back across the room, because the battery was dying, and along the balcony and down the stairs.

Cars were solid in painted slots, and the moonlight bounced from their roofs. And none of the cars had their headlights on.

She found her own car in the row of cars, and it, save for moonlight on its roof, glittering from its windows, was as dark as the others. She tried the door on the right and it was locked. She went around the quiet, dark car and tried the driver's door. It opened to her pull on the handle.

She pressed the plunger under the window and pressed the button in the handle and closed the door. It locked as it was supposed to lock. She tried it and walked a few feet away and went back and tried it again. The door was locked. It hadn't been; now it was.

My car keys, she thought and, once more, ran her way back to the concrete staircase to the balcony and ran up the stairs, holding to the iron railing. When she tried to unlock her door, the key to it trembled in her hand and scraped on metal as she sought the keyhole. But then she found it and the key turned in the lock, and she walked back into light and warmth.

Her handbag was on the bed Toby had left for her. Her car keys were in the handbag.

The lights were not the lights of my car, she thought and sat down, dropped down, into one of the chairs. They were, as I thought at first, the lights of another car which had pulled in beside mine. It was a big black car. I remember that now. But there were no splashes of red on the right front fender. If there had been, I would have seen them. Or—or would I have imagined them? Did I imagine them before? Yesterday. It must have been yesterday.

She got up from the chair and went into the bathroom and ran water cold and splashed it on her face. She looked at her wet face in the mirror and thought, My eyes are wider than they ever are. My eyes stare back at me.

Again she splashed water on her face, but she did not look again into the mirror. She dried her face and thought, My movements are jerky. Uncertain. Or do I imagine that, as perhaps I am imagining other things? But Dr. Strom said that everything would—

She went back to the chair and lighted a cigarette, but then, almost immediately, she got up from the chair and put ice into a glass and poured from her bottle of martinis. She almost never drank after dinner; she had never drunk a martini after dinner. Nobody drinks martinis after dinner. No balanced person. No sane person.

She smoked and sipped, and after a time her mind grew more quiet. Still she was not sleepy. I will sit here until I am sleepy. Perhaps I will turn on the television. But the television set seemed far away across the big room. Too far away to be worth the trouble. Nothing now is worth the trouble. I will sit in this chair and in the room's warmth, and after a while I will get up and go to bed. After—

She felt herself slipping into sleep and thought, I must get up and go to bed because now I am not worried any more, not frightened any more. It was lights on the car next to mine—on the big black—

She heard music and it wakened her. But there could not be music. She had thought about turning the television on, but she had not turned it on. The television screen was featureless, unlighted in the lighted room. But the music continued.

The music was coming through one of the walls. That was all it was. Somebody in the room next to hers had his TV set turned on, and the music from it was coming through her wall and into her room.

It was bright, gay music, not music to sleep by. It was—

It was suddenly loud in her ears and in her mind. It was "Love's the Shortest Distance Between Two People."

Ben had always wanted that played. They could never play it too often. "What shall I put on, Ben?" It was always "Love's the Shortest Distance." Even if they had had it the night before. "Let's play it again. She's marvelous in that. It's a wonderful song. They're both great in that song."

Sometimes he would try to sing it. He couldn't sing and he knew he couldn't, but sometimes he would try to sing "Love's the Shortest Distance Between Two People." I would sing it with him sometimes, though not—of course not—the way she sings it. My voice is all right, but it is a very little voice.

It was strange to hear the song coming through the wall of her room. At first it was a fine song to hear, because it had always been a fine song. At first it brought back, tenderly, evenings—evenings long ago—when evenings in the apartment, with records playing, had been tender evenings. But then the song began to twitch in her mind.

Whoever it is, she thought, is playing his TV much too

( 82 )

loudly. It is time to go to sleep. The walls are too thin to play a TV loudly in a motel room. It's inconsiderate to—

Then she realized that the song had finished but, almost immediately, begun again. What kind of TV program would play a song, even a fine and lilting song, over again just as it was finished? What kind—

She was wide awake, then. She walked across the room to the television set. A notice on it told her that there were three channels available and gave their numbers. She tried them. Two of the programs were of old movies, and she was in the middle of both. The third was a jazz program. Had the Bucci music been earlier on that? It seemed unlikely. The music which came from the television speakers was not Bucci music.

She switched the television off. "—Love's the shortest path in sight" came through the wall. It must, she thought, be for the third time. Whoever it is must—must be playing a phonograph. And when "Love's the Shortest Distance" is finished he lifts the arm and puts the needle back so that the song is played again. Somebody—*somebody is doing it on purpose.* Because whoever it is knows that Ben and I used to play it over and over when Ben was alive. Before Ben jumped from the window and screamed—and screamed —and—

I'll call the office, she thought. I'll tell them that somebody in the room next to mine is playing a phonograph so loudly that I can't sleep. I'll ask them to call the room next to mine and ask whoever's playing records there to cut the volume. It's after ten at night and too late—

She picked up the telephone. It hummed faintly. On this telephone there was no finger-hole marked "Office." She waited for several seconds and the telephone only hummed. Last night Bobby had said that that motel switchboard was cut off at ten. Apparently this one also closed down at night.

I can get something in my hand and pound on the wall, Carol thought. I can call through the wall. I can tell whoever it is that his music is keeping me awake. I can—

But then she realized that "Love's the Shortest Distance"

was no longer coming through her wall. There was quiet in the big room.

She lay on the bed Toby had not chosen and lighted a cigarette and thought, It's just a coincidence. It's a fine song and a lot of people like it. And a lot of people carry phonographs with them when they travel and play records they are fond of. It's—it's not part of anything. It was—it was not meant to disturb me. Whoever was playing records and in the next room, and playing one of them over and over, has never heard of me. There isn't any—any conspiracy against me, any plot to harass me. The car with the red splashes on its right front fender was not following me, marked so that I would know it was. None of the other things—

A word came into her head. The word was "persecution." She tried to push it out, but another word—a word even more disturbing—took its place. The second word was "paranoia."

But I'm not, she told herself. She did not speak aloud but the rejection was loud in her mind. I'm not. I'm *not*.

She turned on her side. She said, aloud this time, "Wake up, Toby. Wake up and talk to me. Wake *up*."

Toby twitched the tip of his long brown tail. He moved one ear slightly toward her. He did not say anything.

She had told herself that morning that she would not again take two sleeping capsules. She took two sleeping capsules. She undressed and got into bed, and after what seemed a long time she went to sleep. She dreamed the lilt of the Bucci song, but nothing wakened her.

Again, it was Toby who wakened—awakened her by standing on her and touching her lips softly with a paw. She said, "Go away, Toby," but Toby did not go away. She got up and fed her cat and dressed and, resolutely, shut all memories, and so far as she could, all thought out of her mind. The lyrics of "Love's the Shortest Distance Between Two People" kept repeating themselves in her mind and they were welcome there because they did not nag in her mind. She walked behind the motel, as she had the night before, and across the street and into the restaurant. "Love's the short-est—"

It was going to be a bright day. Sunlight slanted down on her as she walked back from the restaurant, climbed the cement stairs to the cement balcony. It was warmer than it had been the night before. I won't need my coat in the car today. Perhaps I will not even need the heater on. The South is coming up to meet me.

She carried bags down and Toby's pan and had to put them down on the pavement while she unlocked the car doors. She went back upstairs and got Toby—"Love's the shortest path"—and leashed him in the back seat. Toby spoke about it loudly; he had spoken even more loudly as he was carried downstairs. He did not like to be carried downstairs.

The car which had been next to hers was gone when she got into the Buick. The car which had arrived late and been left for a time with its headlights blazing. Of course it had been the headlights of that car, not of hers. Nobody would have got into her car and turned the lights on and then, later—after she had seen them—turned them off again. There would have been no reason for anybody to do that. No sane reason.

The car started at once when she turned the ignition key. She backed and circled and drove behind the motel and turned on the street she had four times walked across. "—the shortest path—" She waited for lights, and turned south on Market Street, which was Route 17, and drove slowly, often stopped by lights along Third Street, which seemed to be the city's main street, and crossed a bridge, and traffic thinned and her way was on "U.S. 17, South."

("Just follow 17 south from Wilmington. It's slow through Charleston unless they've got the new bypass finished. Be sure to take the bypass around Savannah. 17A I think it is. It's rather a long day to Brunswick, but that's where the next Stetson Lodge is. When Bill and I stop there we always go to a restaurant called The Deck. It's very good, we both think. We always eat in the bar.")

( 85 )

She tried to keep the lyrics in her mind, to keep meaningless—imagined—fears out of it. But the lyrics slipped out of her mind. I'm not paranoid. I'm not. I'm not. I looked it up once. What did it say? Delusions. "Systematized delusions." I think that was what it said. Something or other "ascribed to the supposed hostility of others." That was what it said. Why did I look it up? Oh—I thought people were against me at the office. I asked Dr. Strom. And he only laughed at me. And said—oh, that there was enough real hostility in the world so that it wasn't necessary to make it up. He told me not to worry about myself. He told me I was all right.

I was just tired and worried when I started this long drive day before yesterday. Jangled because of the awful thing that happened. (Ben screamed so, *screamed* so.) And pulled down, physically and every other way, by this cold which I could not shake off.

It was a long day. She crept through the back streets of Charleston—narrow streets through what must be the worst part of a gracious city. Following the "17" signs through Charleston took her through nothing gracious. It also demanded the most complete attention, leaving no room in the mind for anything but traffic lights and cars which almost scraped hers and bedraggled dogs running loose in traffic.

She did not miss the bypass around Savannah in midafternoon. "Brunswick, 75 miles." "Brunswick, 50 miles." "Brunswick City Limits; Speed Laws Enforced." A western hat with lights twinkling its shape. "Room One eleven, Mrs. Sanders. It's one of our nicest rooms. You're well back from traffic. Alfred, show Mrs. Sanders where One eleven is." A restaurant called The Deck? "Six blocks down the highway. There's a sign. You can't miss it. It's on your left. You have to make a little zigzag. Otherwise you get the wrong way in a one-way road."

Again, as on the night before, she climbed cement stairs in the rear of a building. This time the windows of her big room looked out on grass and trees and on a swimming pool, drained for the winter. And on the grinding highway beyond.

This time her room had a little balcony of its own. There were two directors' chairs on the little balcony. This time, after Alfred had opened the French doors to the little balcony and brought her ice and said, "Thank *you*, miss. Is there anything else, miss?" she went out onto the little balcony.

It was not cold there; she had left the cold behind. She could look down on palm trees, which appeared to be having a tough time of it. She could look down on lights. But it was not warm enough to sit on the little balcony, and she went back into the room and closed the French doors and drew curtains across the doors and the windows which flanked them.

The rest was not too different. The two beds were three-quarter beds, not double beds. The TV set was placed so that one could lie on either of the beds and look at it. Toby found the bathroom and came back to tell her, loudly, that it was dinnertime. He ate his dinner; she could hear him scratching in his toilet pan. He scratched long, having long observed restraint, as cats will when things about them are unfamiliar.

She wrestled a glass out of its hygienic wrapping and put ice in it and poured mixed martini on the ice and sat in a low chair and stretched slim, stiffened legs out in front of her. It was seven o'clock then. It had been a long day, as Maude had told her it would be. It had been a day when her car started readily; a day in which no special car had followed her over the miles. She smoked and sipped from her glass and thought about going out again and driving six blocks in traffic to a restaurant called The Deck.

There was a Howard Johnson's in the motel grounds. She could walk to it; not drive the car again, make a left turn through traffic; zigzag to avoid the wrong way in a one-way road. The food would be all right. Not exciting, but all right. She—

The telephone rang. She jumped and relaxation broke into bits in her mind. A little of the drink had spilled from her glass. She put the glass down slowly, carefully, on the splattered table. She thought, I don't have to answer it. Nobody knows I am here; it won't be for me. I don't have to answer it. Nobody knows—

But that was, she realized, not entirely true. Maude Hudson had been scrupulous in her directions; she had mentioned this Stetson Lodge in Brunswick as a good one to stop at. It might be Maude calling—calling to tell her that something had happened in Vero? Something that could change her plans?

The telephone kept on ringing. It seemed to Carol that there was impatience in its ringing.

She got up slowly, felt her mind tighten. She walked slowly across the room and picked the telephone up and said, "Yes?"

"Mrs. Sanders?"

"Yes."

"This is the office, Mrs. Sanders. You did ask about going to The Deck for dinner?"

"Yes."

"The thing is, there seems to have been an accident down there and they say the road is blocked. I just thought you ought to know. Probably they've got it all cleared up now, but I thought you ought to know."

"It's good of you," Carol said. "What happened? Was—was it a bad accident?"

"Nobody got hurt, far's I've heard. Car got forced off the road somehow. Making the turn, I shouldn't wonder. In the wrong lane, I shouldn't wonder. Anyway, Ned Bromley—he's a trooper we know—says the road's blocked. I just thought you ought—"

"Yes," Carol said. "This car that was forced off the road. Did Mr. Bromley tell you what kind of car it was? What make, I mean?"

"Yes'm. He says it was one of those little Buicks with the big engine. A Sky-something."

"Skylark," Carol said, with numbness in her voice. "What they call a Gran Sport, if it had the big motor. Was a woman driving it, did this trooper say?"

( 88 )

"Yes," the office said. "One of our guests, actually. Reason Ned came to tell us about it. Brought her back here in his cruiser, Ned did. She's all right. Shook up, but all right. Pretty little thing."

"The car that forced her off the road," Carol said. "Was it—"

"Just went on, Ned says. Didn't even stop to see what'd happened. Some of these drivers!"

"Yes," Carol said.

"Because you asked about The Deck," the office—which was female—said. "I thought you ought to know about the accident."

"Yes," Carol said. "It was very thoughtful of you. I'm glad the girl's all right."

"Just shaken up, like I said. Crying and everything. But she says she's all right. And that it was the other car was going the wrong way. A big black car she says it was. Which, like Ned says, doesn't get anybody anywhere."

"No," Carol said, "I can see it doesn't. Thank you for calling me. I'll—probably I'll just walk over to the Howard Johnson's."

"It's a good restaurant," the office said. "It was just that you asked about The Deck, Mrs. Sanders. They don't serve drinks at the Howard Johnson's but the food's right good."

Carol said she was sure it was. And again she said, "Thank you," and hung up. And she went, still very slowly, back to her chair and her drink. She had left a cigarette burning in the tray. It was now only a long gray ash. Toby had changed his mind about beds. He was curled up in her chair. He said "Yooow-*ow*" when he was lifted out of it. When she put him on her lap he jumped down again at once and picked out his bed.

She lighted a cigarette and tinkled ice in her glass and drank. This time she did not merely sip; this time she swallowed. The drink was harsh in her throat. It made her cough. The cough was, of course, part of the cold's persistence.

That the car which had been forced off the road somewhere near a restaurant called The Deck was a car like hers was a coincidence. It did not mean anything. It was not a part of anything—not part of a sequence of things. A woman had been driving the car. "A pretty little thing." That had nothing to do with anything. I'm little, Carol thought. Men have called me "pretty." That has nothing to do with anything.

Buick Skylarks, GS or not, come in a good many colors. Probably the car which was forced off the road was a red car, or a blue car. Not a white car with a black top, like mine. It was a car nobody, parked here waiting, could have mistaken for my car—could have followed, by mistake, and forced off the road. It is true that a woman was driving this other car—a young woman, a "pretty little thing." But she was not forced off the road because somebody thought she was me.

She finished her drink, stubbed her cigarette out. I'll go to the restaurant, she thought. Go where there are other people. Driving so far alone, with nobody to talk to except my cat—who sleeps most of the time; talks back only when he happens to feel like it—erodes the mind. It empties the mind, leaving it a cavern for meaningless, ugly fantasies.

But when she stood up, intending to put on a face to show to people in a restaurant, her legs felt stiff again, and she was, momentarily, uncertain on them. Instead of putting on a face, she put more ice in her glass and again poured martini on it. She was careful about the amount, although the first drink seemed to have had no effect. She went back to the chair and sat in it and lighted another cigarette and sipped from her glass.

I am putting it off, she thought. I know I should go out where other people are, where quite ordinary people are; people who stop at Howard Johnson's restaurants for dinner and for all those kinds of ice cream. Young people and old people and people with children; people who are driving north or driving south, and people who live here in Brunswick, Georgia, and have dinners out at Howard Johnson's. I should go out and listen to other voices and let them replace the voices in my mind.

She drank again and listened to the voices which were only in her mind. I am putting it off, one of the voices said, because, suddenly, I am afraid of people. Because whoever drove the car which followed me down the Jersey Turnpike may be one of the people; the man who telephoned me, using Ben's voice, may be one of the people in the restaurant. Because—

She emptied her glass and, again, crushed out her cigarette. When she got up this time it was to move quickly—to strip off the clothes she had driven in, to shower—ending with cold water which might shock her mind back into reason. She dressed in fresh clothes and did her face and brushed her crisp, short brown hair.

Toby sat up on his bed and looked at her. "Do I look all right, Toby?" she asked her cat. "Am I somebody you can be proud of?"

Toby did not say anything. He began to wash up. He wants to be as clean and fresh as I am, she thought. He's a good cat. He's a fine cat. "Take care of yourself, Tobermory." It was a time to use the full name of her cat. Toby scratched behind his right ear. "Stay right there, Tobermory. I'll be back very soon. Don't let anybody—" She broke that off. "Don't hide under things and worry me."

Toby twitched the end of his tail. He turned around twice and curled.

She put on the loose coat and dropped the doorkey in one of its pockets. She went out and down the cement stairs and stopped at her black and white car. She had not locked the car doors. She locked them. She went through a passageway and walked along a path to the restaurant. She passed a dozen cars, nosed in front of motel rooms. None of them was a black car with a paint-smeared right fender. Of course none was. That car was hundreds of miles away. It was in its garage in Baltimore or in Washington. It had gone to the west; it was in Pennsylvania; it had gone on south. It was in Virginia. It—

There were people in the restaurant, but not as many as she had expected. She looked at her watch. It was eight-thirty, which was late for having dinner in a roadside Howard Johnson's. Her table was by the window; she could look out and watch traffic, streaming north and streaming south. All of the cars and trucks seemed to be going very fast. But when one sits by the roadside and watches cars passing they always seem to be passing at great speed.

A waitress said, "Good evening, miss," and put a menu in front of her. She ordered. When the food came she ate. She lingered for a little while over coffee and a cigarette and looked around her at the people—at a heavy bald man wearing a jacket over a sports shirt; at the woman across from him who was wearing a mink stole and loops of necklace and red hair which had, Carol thought, planned another color for itself. A small boy came and stood beside her table and said, "I had a chocolate ice cream."

"That's nice," Carol said. "Was it good?"

"It was all right, I guess," the boy said. "I like strawberry better."

There seemed to be no reasonable answer to this except, "Do you?"

A young woman in slacks which clung tight to her, not greatly to her advantage, took the boy firmly by the arm and said, "Don't bother the lady, Ronald," and then, "He's really just friendly, miss."

"Of course," Carol said. "He didn't bother me. He's a very nice boy."

"Sometimes," the young woman said. "Come on, Ronny."

"Dessert, miss?"

Carol shook her head. She picked up the check the waitress left and looked at it and put coins down and went to the desk and paid. She went out of the restaurant. It was warmer, she thought, than it had been when she went in. The moon, which was not as round as it had been the night before, was just showing above the motel roof. It was a hazy moon.

Carol started across the paved area between the restaurant and the motel. A car beeped at her, gently, and she moved aside out of its way. It went slowly toward the mo-

( 92 )

tel, as if feeling its way. It paused and the man driving it, who wore a coverall with words "BERT'S GARAGE" stenciled on it, took a slip of paper out of his pocket and looked at it and put it back in his pocket. He turned the car a little to the left, then, and nosed it in between two other cars. He got out of it and walked toward the motel office.

The car he got out of was a white Buick Skylark with the letters "GS" on its tail. It was a white car with a black top. Its right front fender was crumpled.

The little car had New York State license plates. The number began with a V. Mine has a N in it, Carol thought. That's the only difference. My license number has an N in it and hers has a V.

Otherwise, the cars are twins, she thought. Anybody could take one for the other. Anybody could make a mistake and think this car was mine. It wouldn't have had a crumpled fender when it left here and was driven toward this restaurant called The Deck.

A short tunnel led her through the motel building toward the staircase she must climb. It was a brightly lighted tunnel, but it seemed long as she walked through it. I am walking very slowly because I want to run, Carol thought.

She walked slowly up the cement stairs and slowly along the balcony to the door marked "111." The key in her fingers fumbled for the keyhole.

She had left the lights on. It was bright inside—bright and warm. Toby was curled on the bed where she had left him. He looked up at her and the tip of his tail twitched, but he didn't say anything. . . .

She dreamed she was driving the black and white Buick on a narrow, twisting road. In the dream a big black car came toward her, in the middle of the road, and there was not room to pass and she turned to the right and went into a ditch and up against something, and there was the sound of rending metal. The big black car did not stop. It was driven by a man who wore a coverall and something over his face. His window was open and he called to her through it.

( 93 )

He called, "Turn your lights on. You'll run your battery down." In the dream he called to her with Ben's voice.

The dream did not waken her, except enough to make her grope in her mind and find the dream and tell it that it was only a dream—an ugly dream. Then she slept again.

It was Toby who wakened her, as before by standing on her and putting a soft paw against her face. She said, "Go away, Toby," and then, with eyes open and sleep gone, she said, "It's still dark, Toby. It isn't time to get up."

But then she looked at her watch and saw that it was almost eight o'clock, which was later by an hour than she had meant it to be. It was too dark for it to be so late. She had drawn the curtains—she was sure she had drawn the curtains—before she went to bed, but they had not been curtains heavy enough to shut off morning's light. It should not be so dark in the room. There should be sunlight trickling in.

With his mission accomplished, Toby jumped from the bed and said, rather loudly, that he was hungry. Carol got more slowly from the bed. She turned on the light by it and then crossed the room and pulled the cord which should open the curtains she had drawn together. The curtains opened. She looked out into dense fog, in which lights were faint, seemed drowned.

She fed Toby; she dressed; she put Toby's harness on and leashed him to a chair leg. When she put her coat on she pulled it tight around her, belted it tight.

The air was a cold, wet blanket around her as she went through the tunnel and across to the restaurant. A good many of the cars which had been nosed in in front of the motel had gone. The black and white Buick with its battered fender was still where the garage man had put it.

It was brighter in the restaurant, and she got the table she had had the evening before. The cars on the highway had their lights on. They were going much more slowly than they had gone the night before. They were sounding their horns at one another.

"Good morning, miss," the waitress said. "Not that it's

much of one, is it? We get them here this time of year." She put a menu down in front of Carol and Carol pushed it away. "Just toast and coffee," Carol said.

"No juice?"

The tone was disapproving. "All right," Carol said. "Orange juice."

She did not want to argue about anything. For breakfast, people had juice. The custom was inviolable. She could not, this gray morning, set herself against custom.

"And juice," the waitress said, her tone approving. She went away.

The small boy who had come the evening before to tell her he had had chocolate ice cream came back. "I had oatmeal. Mama makes me have oatmeal."

"Because it's good for you," Carol said, and then remembered the small boy's name and added, "Ronald."

"Ronny," the boy said. "My name's Ronny."

The young woman in the slacks which were too tight for a bulging rump came and took the boy rather abruptly by the hand and said, "You mustn't bother the lady, Ronald." She took him away.

Carol drank orange juice, which was very cold, and drank coffee, which was very hot, and ate toast which, a little disconsolately, split the difference. She went back through the fog, her coat tight around her. The fog was heavy on the waiting Buick; the windshield was opaque with fog. She carried things down to the car and carried Toby down. Toby said again, loudly, that he did not like to be carried down stairs.

When she got into the car it was a gray cavern. It took what seemed to be a long time for the engine to catch. But that was only because the points were wet. The starter was resolute. The motor succumbed to revolution and roared at her.

She could not see through the windshield; the mirror reflected the gray blankness of the rear window. She turned the heater on and set the other lever to "Defrost." Cold air came up around her; windshield glass and window glass remained opaque. She remembered then. "You can get a mix," the salesman had told her—had told her and Ben when they were buying the little car. He had told them how to get a mixture—warm air and dry air.

For some seconds, while the engine roared at her, she could not remember what she had to do. She thought, The fog is in my mind, as it is in the air. Then she remembered. She pushed one lever up from "Defrost" to "AC." She pulled the other down to "Hot."

For almost a minute, little came of this. Then air began to come out of vents and the air grew warm. And, slowly, the wet grayness faded from windshield and windows. She set the wipers going and backed out and circled and drove past the Howard Johnson's. She turned her lights on high and glare bounced off the fog and back into her eyes. She dipped the lights and waited her chance and got onto Route 17, South. When she edged into the southbound lane a car honked at her angrily although she had not impeded it or endangered it. Driving in fog makes people nervous.

She found a niche in the southbound traffic. The car behind her had its lights on full, and they dazzled in her mirror. She turned the knob on the mirror, and the lights behind dimmed and seemed to become more distant. But they remained bright, glaring, in the side mirror. Her own dipped lights seemed to skim on the pavement's wetness.

She drove slowly; when a chance offered she got into the right-hand lane. Her lights picked up "Downtown Brunswick" and an arrow which twisted to the right. She slowed, and the car behind blared at her.

That would be wrong, she thought. Downtown would be wrong. Her lights picked up "17, South," and an arrow pointing toward the grayness of the sky. She went ahead. She went across a bridge and kept right, as a sign instructed. Traffic thinned around her. "Two Way Traffic Ahead. Keep Right." She edged almost to the shoulder and dropped her speed to thirty. Her lights groped into the fog and died in it.

The lights of northbound cars were dim and came out

( 96 )

of the fog without warning. There would be nothing coming toward her. Then, seemingly only feet away, there would be car lights. In spite of herself, she cringed toward the right as each pair of lights showed through the fog. The road curved. Then it straightened. She picked up speed a little, but only to forty.

Lights were dim in the mirror in front of her. Then they were bright, glaring, in the side mirror.

The car behind her was pulling out to pass. As it came into clearer sight in her mirrors, swerving out, the lights of an approaching car nudged out of the fog. He'll never make it, Carol thought and then, Shall I slow to give him room ahead of me, or speed up so that he can drop back? Because the three of us are going to smash into each other and—

The approaching car swerved to the right, onto the shoulder. But the car which had been about to pass and which now, with the other car on the shoulder—and sounding an angry, uninterrupted horn—could have made it, dropped back instead.

As she passed the car which had stopped on the shoulder it continued to blare, in anger and in outrage.

It had cause to, Carol thought. The car behind me must be driven by a crazy person. Only a lunatic would try to pass in fog like this. But even a crazy person can learn. He will have learned from that. He might have killed all of us—himself and me and the frightened, angry people in the other car.

She held the Buick at forty, which was fast enough—which was too fast.

The lights of the following car were still in her mirrors. It was keeping very close; keeping too close. If a car ahead slowed suddenly—slowed to take a side road, or to creep to the shoulder and cower there, waiting for light—the car behind would crash into her as she slowed behind it.

There was no car ahead. Then, in the instant of that realization, there were taillights ahead, dimly red. They seemed very close. She eased down on the brake pedal and slowed to the speed of the car ahead, which was not signaling any turn; which was merely creeping south.

The lights in her mirrors were instantly much nearer. They glared in the side mirror as, again, the following car swerved out to pass.

This time no adverse lights showed ahead. She slowed still further to allow space for the passing car to get in front of her, and behind the creeping car she followed. But, when the passing car was only part of the way into the north-bound lane, it pulled back again behind her.

Three times more, as she went south behind the creeping car, the car whose driver must be mad pulled out to pass and then, twice for no reason apparent to Carol, dropped back again. The other time the reason was apparent. The reason was approaching headlights.

The car never dropped far back—never far enough back. He's tailgating, Carol thought. He's a frightening driver; he is reckless and he cannot make up his mind. He ought to be—something ought to be done about drivers like that. They ought to be taken off the road. They ought to be taken off the road and locked up somewhere. She trundled south, and anger, mixed with fear, rode with her.

It was after ten when she realized that her lights were reaching farther into the fog. Then, slowly, there was a luminous texture to the fog. The lights of approaching cars no longer appeared suddenly ahead, and they were brighter lights. Then a car coming toward her had no lights at all. She could see it when it was, at a guess, a quarter of a mile away.

She drove into watery sunlight. The car ahead picked up speed and she matched her own speed with it. Then the taillights ahead went out and the sun was bright on the roadway. She cut her own lights. The wipers squealed on dry glass and she turned the wipers off.

She looked into the mirror above the dashboard. It showed, far back, a following car. It was a little car. She thought it was a Volks. But the car behind was a big car, she thought. It was tailgating me. When it was not making those foolish, abortive, efforts to get ahead of me. It was a black car. A big black car. It must have turned off somewhere. When the fog lifted, it must have turned off.

( 98 )

# 7 ～

She drove out of Georgia into Florida. Except that the road surface changed, there didn't seem to be much difference. She passed a tourist information center. There was a difference. Around the low stucco buildings with tile roofs, palm trees grew tall and were green. There had been palms in Brunswick, but they had looked a little tired of being there.

The sun beat down on the car, which now, with the road straight ahead, was a hurrying car. She pulled a sun shield down, but the sun was hot on her knees. She turned the heater off, but the car still grew warmer. She pressed the knob at her side and the window opened a little. Noise rushed into the car but air came with it, and the air was warm.

She could go around Jacksonville on a bypass road. Maude had written her that in the most explicit letter of direction—a letter written, Carol had amusedly thought, for the benefit of a person who could not be expected to be able to read maps. The bypass road was 95 or 1A or something; anyway, it was marked clearly enough. "You can't miss it," Maude had written, blithely, if unconvincingly, assuring.

A filling station showed up ahead, on the right. Carol looked at her gauge. It showed a quarter. The little Buick's big engine was a thirsty engine. (*Consumer Reports* had mentioned that, and also that it had more power than anybody would ever need. Ben had been firm in rejecting that. "Pickup," he had said. "They never realize that you need pickup.")

She pulled into the service station and ran the window farther down. The air which came in through it was warm air. The attendant confirmed what the air said for itself. "Warming up," the attendant told her. "Must be getting cold up north. Fill her up, miss?"

He was told to fill her up. He was asked to check under the hood. He checked and banged the hood down. He ran a squeegee over the windshield, erasing the streaks where the wipers had not reached. The road which circled Jacksonville?

About five miles down. She couldn't miss it.

The sign said, "To Routes 1 & 95 South." The arrow hooked to the right and she went as the arrow pointed. She went on a wide divided highway and across a toll bridge. Signs and crooked arrows beckoned her to streets she had never heard of. She ignored their summons. Finally a sign said, "Route 1, South. Next Right." Beyond that sign was another, "1A & 95, Keep Left. Jacksonville Beach."

She was in the right-hand lane and stayed there; turned as arrows pointed, reached the crowded breadth of U.S. 1. (And after some miles read, "Jct. 1A & 95.") So her momentary uncertainty at the fork had been needless. "The point," Dr. Strom had told her, "is to make decisions. Don't brood about them. They probably aren't as important as they seem."

She stayed on Route 1 as the sun rose higher, as it began to lower on her right. At Daytona Beach traffic thickened and she crept from light to light. It was almost two o'clock when a restaurant on her right looked like a pleasant restaurant. It also had a sign which read "Cocktails." She turned in there and parked.

Toby, who had had a restful curl on the back seat, wakened when the car stopped. He stood up and arched his back, and scratched at the leather of the seat cushion and yowled. Carol said, "It won't be long now, Toby," and thought, I'm as reassuring as Maude, with probably as little cause, and felt, for the first time since she had been on this troubled journey, like laughing at herself.

She had found a parking place in the shade. She fed Toby, who wasn't as interested as he had said he would be, and ran windows down a little to give him air and got out of the car. It was warm out of the car; far too warm for her loose coat. She put the coat on the front seat and made sure that the doors were locked. She went into the restaurant and found that it was air-conditioned. She had a martini, which was crisply cold and dry, and a sandwich, and when her waitress asked whether she wanted her coffee hot or iced, hesitated a moment gefore saying "Hot, please." She was really getting south.

Fog had followed her south, but she had driven out of fog. Little things had nibbled at her—nibbled in her mind. But they had been meaningless. The driver who had repeatedly tried to pass, and given it up, and tried again was just an uncertain driver whom fog bewildered. Probably before he caught up with her in the fog, he had tried to pass, and failed to pass—or perhaps perilously succeeded in passing —half a dozen other cars.

It was not meant for me, Carol thought, and sipped coffee and drew on a cigarette. None of the things which have happened, or seemed to happen, was meant for me. My nerves have twitched for many weeks. They have twitched fantasies into my mind. That is all it is. I have let phantoms into my mind.

She went out into the sunlight. She got Toby's drinking bowl and went back into the restaurant and poured water into it and carried it back to Toby. Toby smelled it and looked up and said "Yow-ow?" Which meant, she thought, "What's this stuff you're forcing on me?"

She gave him time to drink before she started the car. He didn't drink. He had, however, eaten his lunch. He stood on hind legs and looked out a window. She backed the car out of the space, and Toby didn't approve and said so. But he lay on the seat, belly down and forepaws neatly joined in front of him, and wrapped his tail around him, which was a position of acceptance.

She drove south on U.S. 1. Signs invited her to Interstate 95 and she rejected the invitations. "We always stay on One," Maude had written. "Ninety-five is just fits and starts still. It will be all right, I guess, if they ever get it finished."

Carol, going by fits and stops through Melbourne, creeping from traffic light to traffic light, had moments of doubting Maude's insistence. Interstate 95 was, apparently, a bypassing road. Melbourne was a place which needed bypassing. It was also a very warm place; people in shorts drove in convertibles with tops down. They turned from the main road at signs which said, "To the Beach." They turned into the crowded road and honked at one another. They were, Carol thought, anxiously gay.

But they have not driven many miles, she thought. With miles still to go.

She ran down the windows of the car as she went from light to light. She thought of closing the windows again and turning on the air conditioning. She did not. It was still too soon for that. Hot sunshine, even though it beat on her through the glass of the windshield, was good. It burned away the fog which for so many miles had seemed to cling to her. It was good to feel air blowing on her, even if the air was thick with exhaust fumes.

I should have changed last night in Brunswick, she thought. Changed out of wool into cotton. Or something partly cotton. Almost nothing is really cotton any more. As nothing is really silk any more. Inching from light to light fills the mind with trivia. Welcome the trivia which fills the mind.

Traffic lights became less frequent. Signs which read, "Speed Limit, 30" became "Speed Limit, 40"—became, "Resume Safe Speed." She let the Buick out to a speed which seemed safe to her. The car had other ideas; she kept them curbed.

It was late afternoon and the sun was low when a sign

said, "Vero Beach 20." The low sun dazzled her eyes, and she pulled down both sun shields. "Vero Beach 10" "Vero Beach City Limits." "Beach Area, Turn Left Next Traffic Light." She waited a light out; turned left; followed a narrow, winding blacktop. After a time—"Speed Limit 25"—the road divided into two narrow blacktops. It reunited and crossed a bridge; it divided again. "A1A" and arrows pointing in both directions. "Stop."

She crossed A1A, as Maude had told her to do. At the next corner, she turned right, as Maude had told her to do. There were shops here and motels and, on her left, apparently set far back—too far to see—something called "The Driftwood Inn." She went on, and the shops and motels changed to low houses, all in pastel stucco, all with red tile roofs. At first, these were close together, separated only by carports. Then they were farther apart. Then, on her left as she drifted south on Ocean Drive, there was only the Atlantic Ocean, with white sand sloping down to it.

"There's a wall around us," Maude had written. "You drive between two stone posts. You'll see a sign with our name on it."

The wall was not high; it was red but not the red of brick. Coral? The stone posts, whitewashed, with the globes of lights on their tops, were pillars more than they were posts. It was dusk when she turned in between them. As she turned in, the lights on the pillars went on.

Inside what was a compound, the graveled drive split into thirds—a third of a drive for each of the one-story, stucco houses. (With red tile roofs.) As Carol reached the division in the drive, Maude came out of the house on the right. Her long, lean face was deeply tanned. She wore shorts and a halter, and her arms and legs were the tan of her face. Her eyes were very blue in her brown face, under short-cut hair which seemed more nearly black than Carol had remembered it.

Carol stopped the car and Maude Hudson came up to it, smiling, saying "Darling. Darling *Carol*." She looked in at

Carol, who was unfastening her seat belt. "My *dear*," Maude said. "You must be sweltering in that suit. It's almost *eighty*."

Carol said, "Hi, Maude. I am," and got out of the car. Her legs were stiff; for an instant she was uncertain on the gravel of the drive.

"I know *just* how you feel," Maude Hudson said. "The first thing is a long cold drink. Before we even start to get you settled in."

It was a wonderful idea. Carol said it was a wonderful idea. Toby said, "Yow-ow-ow-ow!" He paused to consider. He amplified. His amplification was, a little unfortunately, something like a growl.

"The dear kitty," Maude said. "Is um hot and tired too?"

Toby said, "Mm-aaah." He almost never got the "mm" into it. "Miaou" was not in his vocabulary, which was extensive. The "mm-aaah" meant that he was displeased. Possibly, Carol thought, taking off her suit jacket and tossing it into the car, because of the "um." Of course, during the time Maude had stayed in the apartment—the bad time— Toby had stayed under things whenever possible. Which meant nothing, except that Toby chose, sometimes irrationally, among humans.

The sun had almost set. But in New York, Carol thought, following Maude Hudson into the low green house, it must be dark by now. The days are longer here in the South.

She followed into a tile-floored room, the tile a deeper green than the green of the house's stuccoed outer walls. The room was a big room. One of the long walls was formed of glass jalousies, tilted so that air came in—air which smelled of the sea a little. (Or, of course, of the beach across the road, on which seaweed was drying.)

"You just sit down and put your feet up," Maude instructed. "I'll get us something cold to drink. Rum Collins? Except that Bill says I'll never learn how to make them right. Or something else? Gin and tonic?"

Carol said that gin and tonic would be fine. She said, "With lots of ice, please." She sat in a low chair and put her feet up on a padded stool. She drew her breath in deeply and let it out slowly.

But then she remembered something and got up again and went through the door Maude had gone through and along a corridor and found Maude in the kitchen, putting ice in glasses on a tray, measuring gin into them.

"It looks wonderful," Carol said. "I wonder if I could have a bowl—just a small bowl—of water? For Toby."

"The poor dear kitty," Maude said. "Of course. Or—whyn't you bring him in? It's cooler in here."

"He'll be all right in the car," Carol said. "He's used to it now. He likes—oh, one thing at a time. We are—you said we were?—going to stay in—" She paused. "My" house? "Ben's" house?

"Of course," Maude said. "In your home, dear. Everything's all ready." She ran water into a green bowl. She said, "There," and gave the bowl to Carol.

Toby was standing on hind legs, looking out the car window. As soon as he saw Carol, he got down to the car seat and began to scratch it. It was leather. His claws bounced off it. He twisted and bit at his harness.

"Very soon, Tobermory," Carol said, and put the water down on the floor of the car where he could reach it. "Very soon you'll be out of it."

"Yah! Yah-ow."

But he got down and smelled the water. Then, to Carol's surprise, he began to lap from the bowl. He must have got hot in the car. He was not by habit a water drinker—except, of course, of water flowers had stood in.

She went back into the cool house. A tall glass was on a little table by the chair she had been sitting in, and she sat again and put her feet up again. Maude, in a chair opposite hers, with a drink beside that chair, smiled at her. It was a thin-lipped smile. I never noticed how thin her lips are, Carol thought. Of course, when we were in the apartment I didn't notice much of anything.

Again she drew breath in deep. This time she let it out with a sigh.

"Yes," Maude said, "it is good to relax, isn't it? Even if you do it in four days, the way you did, it's a long drive. It was all right? I mean, nothing happened?"

"Just that it was long," Carol said. She reached into her handbag on the floor beside her and fished cigarettes out of it. She lighted a cigarette—Maude got half out of her chair and picked up a folder of matches before Carol held her lighter in view and snapped flame from it.

"The last time Bill and I drove down," Maude said, "we ran into some of the *craziest* drivers. I don't mean we actually ran into them. But we were behind a car and all at once—"

A near catastrophe was detailed. A driver had, belatedly, seen a restaurant he liked and had, abruptly, slowed, without signaling and—if Bill hadn't been as good a driver as he always was—

"We've never driven down that I can remember without little things happening," Maude said. "Not that we've ever had an accident. You were lucky, dear."

"Oh," Carol said. "There were little things. Nothing as—as bad as this man who didn't signal he meant to turn. Nothing as tangible." She paused. She sipped from her long, cold drink and drew on her cigarette. And all the little things, the intangible things, came uneasily back into her mind.

"One gets tired driving," she said and spoke, at first, as much to herself as to the woman with the long tanned face who sat opposite her. "The mind gets tired, I suppose. Gets to imagining things."

Maude raised her eyebrows and then shook her head, and there was an invitation in both movements. And, relaxed with her drink, with the comfortable freedom of her legs, cramped into position for so many miles, Carol went on, not this time to herself. ("Don't keep things bottled up," Dr. Strom had told her. "If you feel like spilling things out, spill them out.")

"The first day on the turnpike," Carol said, "I got the notion that somebody—"

She told of the car with the red-splotched fender.

"*Goodness*," Maude said. "How—how upsetting for you,

dear. But he did turn off? You must just have imagined he was following you."

"Yes," Carol said. "I said it was just a notion. I said the mind gets tired and—and full of fancies."

"You said, 'imagining *things,*'" Maude told her. "As if there had been other—things. Things that troubled you."

"A few," Carol said. "But I'm here safe now. And it's a lovely house, Maude. And a fine drink. I'm fine now."

"Other cars followed you? Or you thought they did?"

("Spill things out," Dr. Strom had said. "If things worry you, talk about them.")

The car she had thought was following her had not been. It had turned off. That was clearer now she had told Maude about it. It no longer nagged in her mind. That was what Dr. Strom had meant; what he had known would happen.

"Tuesday morning," Carol said. "This is Thursday, isn't it? One loses track of days."

"I know," Maude said. "I *always* do. Yes, dear, this is Thursday."

"Then it was Tuesday morning the battery was down," Carol said. "I thought the motor'd never start. But it did. I was sure I hadn't left the lights on and I—I made up crazy stories to explain why the battery was down. But probably I did leave the lights on. Sometimes I do."

"Sometimes everybody does," Maude said. "You said crazy stories. That you made them up. What were they, dear?"

"Only one, really," Carol said, and told of that. Maude said, "Goodness! Why *would* anyone?"

"Nobody did, of course," Carol said. "I forgot to put the lights off. I know that."

It did not work as well this time. Suddenly, quite clearly, she could remember pushing on the plunger which turned off the lights in the Buick. When the boy who took her bags in had been named Bobby.

"That was all it was," Carol said to Maude Hudson. "I forgot to turn the lights off and the battery ran down."

She drank more deeply from her glass. She drew hard on her cigarette and then put it out.

"I've been under strain for a long time," she said. "Since Ben—"

"Of course, dear. Of course you have. What you need is a good long rest. Just to lie in the sun and swim and—and not think about things. Worry about things."

"Yes," Carol said. "And what I need now is a shower and to get out of these clothes and—"

"Of course you do, dear," Maude said. "We'll go over to your house and get you settled in. And then you'll come back here and I'll fix us something to eat. Just for the two of us."

Carol finished her drink. Then the words reached her. "Just the two of us? Not Bill?"

"But I wrote you, dear," Maude said. "Last week, I'm sure it was. That Bill so wanted to be here to meet you and was so sorry he had to fly out to California with Felix. And Vinnie too, as it turned out. There's something about the plant out there. Bugs in something, Bill says. He's always saying there are bugs in things."

"I'm sorry," Carol said. "I've been wanting to meet your husband. And Felix too, of course."

"And you never have," Maude said in a tone of sympathy. "Bill wanted to come up for—when dear Ben—" she took a final sip of her long drink. "But he just couldn't get away. What with Felix on vacation and everything. That more or less left Bill in charge of things, of course."

"Of course," Carol said, with no inflection in her voice. All at once, there was no inflection left in her mind. There was only weariness.

"What you need," Maude said, "is to get settled in. Come on."

She stood up and Carol stood, and the stiffness was back in her legs. But after a moment it went out of them. They went to her car and, to Carol's vague surprise, Maude locked the house door after them and shook it to make sure the lock had caught. But they were only going a hundred yards or so across the compound; they would never be out of sight of Maude's house.

Toby told them he had been kept waiting too long. From deep down in his throat he told Maude Hudson something else. Carol did not try to translate; cats have unaccountable prejudices and are inclined to express them. Carol drove the car on the gravel drive and into the carport of the pink house Maude told her was hers.

The house they carried luggage into was very like Maude's own house—big oblong living room with jalousies along one wall. The ones here were closed. Carol found, vaguely, that she missed something in the immaculate, shining living room. Then she realized she missed a fireplace. Of course. This far down the Florida peninsula there would be no need for fireplaces. There was a big air-conditioning unit, not turned on. "It heats, too," Maude told her. "Sometimes it gets almost cold here in January."

There were two bedrooms, one larger than the other. There were two bathrooms, with towels racked in the one which opened off the larger of the bedrooms. Nothing in any of the rooms looked as if it had ever been used. The towels had the symmetry of the untouched. In the shining kitchen it was the same.

"Ben almost never stayed here," Maude told her, as she led the way from room to room, opened closet drawers, introduced Carol to her house. "He was always in New York. But of course you know that, dear."

Carol nodded her head. She knew that. Once or twice the winter before, when damp cold gripped New York, Ben had said, "We ought to go down to Vero." But they never had.

"Now you just take your time," Maude said. "I'll go back and fix us something, and you come whenever you're ready."

An hour or so? An hour or so would be fine.

Carol took Toby's harness off and put his pans in the kitchen and food in his feeding pan. He went with her, checking up. He smelled, but did not eat, the junior beef in his feeding pan. He looked at the toilet pan. He scratched behind his right ear and went off to explore the house.

Carol took off her suit skirt and hung it and the jacket in

a big closet. Then, for twenty minutes or so, she lay on the wide bed in the big room. She was not hungry; she was only tired. She almost drifted into sleep, but roused herself. She got a linen dress out of one of the bags and thought she should unpack the other things and hang them, hoping the wrinkles would shake out. Instead she showered and put on clean things and the blue linen dress. Toby came into the bedroom as she finished and looked at her appraisingly. Then he jumped on the bed and curled for sleep.

"Now, all right, Toby," Carol told her cat. "But not tonight. You wake up too early."

She was about to leave this so-new house when she thought of morning. She would want breakfast in the morning. She went to the kitchen and found, in refrigerator, on shelves, everything she would need.

There were three doors in the kitchen walls—the one she had come through and, more or less opposite it, another. She opened that one and looked out and looked into a patio with a palm tree in it, and two lounging chairs and privacy insured by hedges. She closed the door and made sure it was locked and opened the third door, in the side wall of the kitchen.

It opened to a small bedroom, with a single bed against one wall. Meant as a maid's room? Meant—

What she saw interrupted the curiosity vaguely in her mind. What she saw was that the narrow bed had been slept in—slept in and left unmade. A sheet and a blanket were tossed back as if somebody had just got out of the bed. The pillow was still dented by a head.

At the end of the bed there was a door. She crossed the narrow room and opened it. It did not open on the patio. It opened on a narrow gravel drive which, she suspected, provided a delivery passage to the house. And, of course, a way in and out for whoever used the room. A servant who slept in? But the house had been, so far as she knew, long unoccupied. Perhaps the Hudsons or Felix and Vinnie Sanders sometimes used the house for overflow guests? Perhaps Maude had hired somebody to clean the house before Carol moved into it, and the cleaning woman had stayed overnight? And gone without remembering to straighten the room she had slept in?

Carol, back in the narrow bedroom, closed the door to the outside and pressed a button in its knob to lock it. She turned the knob and the button in it clicked out. She pressed it back again and pulled on the knob without turning it. The door was locked.

But she was sure—was almost sure—that when she had turned the knob to open the door there had been no click, no popping out of a button on the knob.

Forgotten to lock the door as she left the room? As she had forgotten to strip the bed and smooth a cover over it?

Automatically, Carol spread up the bed, made it neat.

It's just as well I decided to check the kitchen, Carol thought. And found this room with its unlocked outside door. It's all puzzling; it is unlike the way Maude would let things happen. When she was in the apartment with me in New York she always made so sure we locked the door after us when we went out. She was always saying, "You're sure you locked the door, dear?" And just now she locked her own house door when we were only going across the compound.

She'll be upset by this when I tell her, Carol thought. But I'd better tell her.

She put a light coat on over the linen dress and walked, on grass, avoiding the harshness of gravel, from her pink house to Maude and Wilbur Hudson's green house.

# 8 ~

But it couldn't be, Maude told her. It simply *couldn't* be. The room next to the kitchen had been planned by Ben when he built the house as a maid's room. There was a small bathroom—a shower-size bathroom—off it. Had Carol noticed that?

Carol, sipping a martini—with a little too much vermouth in it—shook her head.

"But he was never here enough to have a servant live in the room," Maude said. "As far as I know the bed was never made up in there. Never even had sheets put on. Are you sure, dear?"

"Yes," Carol said. "There were sheets on the bed. And a spread over them. And a case on the pillow. And somebody had slept in the bed. And I think—I'm not sure but I think —the outside door was unlocked."

Maude couldn't understand it. She simply couldn't understand it.

"I had Millie—she works for all of us, you know—clean the house yesterday," Maude said. "So it would be all ready for you. But she wouldn't have slept there, dear. She just comes for the day. She's got her little car and she drives over from wherever she lives. Over off Route One, I think it is. She never stays overnight. *Never!*"

"Somebody did last night," Carol said. "Or the night before."

Again, Maude didn't understand it.

"There wasn't anything to show somebody had broken in?" Maude said. "I mean—a broken window or anything like that? Or marks on the door where somebody had pried it open? With what they call a jimmy?"

"No, Maude."

"Then somebody must have had a key," Maude said, on a note of discovery. "But nobody could have. I had only the one, and that's the one I gave you. It fits all the outside doors. I suppose Ben had one, of course. Didn't he?"

"I don't know," Carol said. "There were a good many keys. They—they didn't have labels on them. But yes, Maude, somebody must have had a key."

"Of course," Maude said, "Millie has a key. She has keys to all three houses so she can get in if we're not home." Maude was, Carol realized, a person who made things clear. "But Millie's honest," Maude said. "I'll give her that." There was an implication that there were other things Maude Hudson would not give her cleaning woman.

"Unless—" Maude said and let it hang and drank from her glass. She was drinking Scotch. She had had some trouble finding the vermouth for Carol's martini. ("Most people around here just drink Scotch. Oh, some of them bourbon.") She put her glass down on the table by her chair.

"Sometimes," she said, "when Millie isn't feeling well she sends a niece of hers as a substitute. A rather pretty little thing. I suppose she lets her niece have the keys to the houses. Only Millie's come herself for weeks and weeks. She came yesterday. Cleaned for me and then crossed to your house and went over it. Of course—"

She paused again. She drank again, finishing her drink.

"I suppose it's possible," she said, and spoke slowly. "Possible this niece of hers has got mixed up with that crazy crowd over on A One A. Hippies or yippies or whatever they call themselves. I wouldn't put anything past them. Perhaps this niece of Millie's let one of them copy the key when she had it. That might explain it, I suppose. Only—"

She shook her head.

"They've got a place of their own," Maude said and looked thoughtfully at her empty glass. "The old Sanford place a few miles down A One A. Rented it, I guess. It's more or less falling down. Nobody has lived in it for years, they say. But I don't suppose that would bother these crazy kids."

"Hippies?" Carol said. "Down here?"

"It's a good climate," Maude said. "Last month, when it was warmer at nights than it is now, they went over on the beach at nights. They played guitars and things and sang songs and—oh, just sort of danced around. Without any clothes on, I shouldn't wonder. One night Bill called the police and they sent a car. But the sergeant came over and said there wasn't anything to do about them, because they weren't really making enough noise to be called disturbing the peace and there wasn't, so far as he could see, any more indecent exposure than there usually is on beaches. And that all beaches in Florida are supposed to be public."

She got up and lifted her glass from the table.

"It is upsetting," she said. "I'm going to have another short one before I put the steak on. And there's a dividend for you in the shaker."

Which, Carol thought, probably has been standing on ice for the last half hour. Which may, I suppose, dilute the vermouth. What she said was, "That'll be fine, Maude."

Maude went out to the kitchen. She returned with a filled glass for herself and a martini mixer, half full of liquid and ice, for Carol. She poured from the mixer into Carol's empty glass—an old-fashioned glass, because there hadn't been any cocktail glasses around. The drink had stood on ice for at least half an hour. It still tasted of vermouth.

"Only," Maude said, "why use the room in your house, Carol? When they've got this place of their own? And, why use the little room when, once they were inside, they could have used any of the rooms?"

"I don't know," Carol said. "I don't think there was more than one. It looked—well, as if there had been only one head on the pillow. When I spread up the bed again."

"Oh," Maude said. "You made the bed?"

"It was—oh, automatic," Carol said. "I've never been able to stand unmade beds."

Maude looked at Carol over her glass. It seemed to Carol that Maude's eyes narrowed in speculation.

"No," Carol said, "I didn't imagine it, Maude. It wasn't —oh, like my imagining a car was following me. Somebody had slept in the bed and just thrown back the sheet and covers when he got out of it." She narrowed her own eyes a little as she looked at Maude Hudson. "I'm sorry I made the bed again," she said, and spoke slowly. "If I hadn't, you could have looked at it yourself, couldn't you? Made sure I hadn't imagined it?"

"My *dear*," Maude said. "What a thing to say! You make it sound as if—*really*, Carol!"

It had, Carol thought, been a bad thing to say. "I'm sorry," she said. "I'm tired and jumpy. I know you don't think I— well, that I made something up. Or imagined it."

"Of *course* I don't," Maude said. "Whatever could have made you think a thing like that?"

Your narrowed eyes, Carol thought. She said, "I don't know. It was a long drive and there were—I thought there were—these little annoying things. It's all left me—oh, jumpy. I'm sorry, Maude. You've done so much to make things right for me here. I'll be fine tomorrow."

"Food," Maude told her. "What you need is food. And to finish your drink. I'll go put the steaks on." She stood up. She said, "How would you like yours, dear?"

"Rare," Carol said. "Oh, however you like it, Maude."

"There are two of them," Maude said. "Quite little ones. I can leave mine in longer."

She went to put steaks on. Or, Carol hoped, under an oven's electric broiler. Carol sipped her dilute drink. Maude came back carrying plates and silver and began to set a table at the far end of the long room. No, there wasn't anything Carol could do. Except just relax and finish her drink. There wasn't really *any*thing to do.

The steaks were good. They had browned under a broiler. Maude had left them both in "a little longer," but Carol's was pinkish under the brown crust. (Maude's appeared to be gray. Rarity in steak is a variable, lodged in the subconscious.) But the steaks were tender, and the peas with them had been picked and frozen when they were still sweet and young peas. The wine was from California, but it was a Samuele Sebastiani Cabernet Sauvignon and good. (It was a wine which, when they had wine with dinner, which was not often, Ben had liked.)

It was relaxing to be at her destination; to know that tomorrow, and the day after tomorrow, she would not have to drive an eager car over many miles of highway. She had not thought herself hungry; she ate with pleasure and sipped the taut wine. Across their little table, Maude smiled at her, and nodded approval of her appetite. The jalousies were still partly open, and the air which came gently through them smelled of the sea. I'm glad I came, Carol thought. I will be all right again here.

They moved back to the other end of the room for coffee and little cookies. Carol's relaxation deepened. It deepened into yawns.

"It's a long drive down," Maude said. "I know how tired you must be. You'll want a long, long sleep."

"Yes," Carol said. "I can use sleep. It's hard to sleep well when you've been driving all day. The first night I dreamed of trucks. And trucks and trucks."

"I know," Maude said. "Bill does all the driving, usually, but I know. And then this car you thought was following you. Did you dream of that? I would have."

"I don't remember," Carol said. "The next night, I think, I dreamed I was lost. Because somebody had stolen the map."

"The map?"

"The one I had marked the routes on," Carol said. "The routes you had written me were the best ones. I thought I put it in the car. I was sure I had. But I guess I forgot to. Anyway it wasn't there. In the car, I mean. That was the day after the battery had run down. Almost down. I told you. I got the crazy idea somebody had got in the car and turned the lights on to run the battery down. And stolen the map."

"Dear," Maude said, "why on earth would anyone? You can get a map at any service station."

"I know," Carol said. She felt she was speaking drowsily. "It was—for a while I thought somebody had done it just—just to badger me. But I just must have forgotten to put it in the car."

"We all forget things. You hadn't told me about the map. Did other things happen? The car that was following you. You told me about that. And the battery, because you forgot to turn off your lights. Were there other things, dear?"

("Don't keep things bottled up. Let them spill out.")

"A girl in a car got sideswiped," Carol heard herself saying. "The car was just like mine—a twin of mine. She was on her way to a restaurant I'd been advised to go to."

"How awful," Maude said. "This girl—was she hurt?"

"Just shaken up," Carol said. "And the car got a dented fender."

"Carol dear," Maude said. Her voice was gentle. But, as before, her eyes seemed to narrow a little. "You didn't think somebody had run into this poor girl on purpose? Thinking —well, thinking he was hitting your car?"

"For a little while. Oh, half thought that. I guess was afraid of that."

Maude shook her head slowly and smiled and shook her head again.

"Dear," she said, "you do let your imagination run away with you. You've been under strain for a long time. That detective who came to see you after Ben—after Ben's accident. Did he bother you any more?"

"He came again," Carol said. She felt the relaxation, the sleepiness, drifting away. "Maude, did you know Ben was—was sick? That he had a brain tumor? Would have had to have had an operation?"

"No," Maude said. "Oh *no. No!*"

"They found out when they did the autopsy," Carol said. "He never told you about it? Wrote you? Or Felix?"

"I didn't know," Maude said. "I'm sure Felix didn't. How dreadful. He—I wish he had told us. He did tell you?"

( 117 )

"No," Carol said. "I didn't know about it until this detective told me. Only that—well, for the last several months he'd not been himself. Not quite himself. Irascible. He had always been gentle before. Considerate. Last summer he began to change. I suppose it was because of this tumor. But he never told me he was sick. Had been to see Dr. Strom."

Maude repeated the name. She made the name sound a question.

"A neurologist," Carol said. "A neurosurgeon. And a psychiatrist. A fine doctor. A very understanding man."

"You sound as if you knew him, Carol. Wait. When Ben wrote us about you. That you and he were going to get married. He said something about your having had a little trouble. But that you were all over it. Did—" She stopped. Then she said, "I shouldn't be asking you this."

But you are, Carol thought, and all relaxation had ebbed away.

"Yes," she said. "I went to see Dr. Strom a few times. But I was all right when Ben and I were married. And—I'm all right now."

"Of course you are. Anybody can see that." She smiled again. Her smile, thin-lipped or not thin-lipped, was a warm and friendly smile. "You're just tired and need a good long sleep." She smiled again. "Only," she said, "I'm afraid all this has waked you up. Bothered you. I'm sorry, dear. So sorry."

"It's all right," Carol said. "It wasn't anything you did, Maude. I—I just got to remembering things, I guess." She looked at her watch, which showed her it was a little after ten. "I am sleepy," she told Maude Hudson, and told herself—insisted to herself. "When you're driving you get in the habit of going to bed early, so you can get up early. Anyway, after dinner there's nothing else to do except look at TV."

(And hear music coming through the wall from the room next to yours, she thought. Familiar music seeping through a thin wall. I won't tell Maude about that. She'd—she'd think it was something else I imagined. Made up.)

She stood up rather quickly and lifted her handbag from

the floor beside her. Maude sat for a moment and then she, too, stood.

"Sleep," Maude said. "That's what you need. Would you like me to walk over with you?"

"No," Carol said. "I can find my way." She took a step toward the door. She turned and said, "It was a fine dinner. You're being very good to me."

"You're family," Maude said. "We want you to be happy here with us. You remembered to bring your key? To your house, I mean?"

"Yes," Carol said. "I don't really often forget things."

"Of course you don't," Maude said and then, unexpectedly, snapped her fingers. She said, "I almost did. Wait a minute, dear."

Carol waited, near the door. Maude was gone for several minutes.

"Forgot where I put it," she said, from the corridor, and then came into the room.

She had a small automatic pistol dangling by its trigger guard from a finger of her right hand.

"Bill said I mustn't forget to give you this," she said. She looked into Carol's face and smiled again. "Not that you'll need it," she said. "But Bill made such a point of it. Because, the way things are nowadays, you can't ever be sure."

"I don't—" Carol said.

"Just so I can tell Bill I didn't forget," Maude said, and held the little handgun out. "Please, Carol. I promised Bill I'd see you took it home with you. All of us down here keep guns in the house. Just to be sure."

Carol took the gun in her hand. It felt strange in her hand.

"Do you know how to use it?"

"I've never used a gun in my life," Carol said. "Any kind of gun."

"It's very easy," Maude said. "You just point it and pull the trigger. With the safety off, of course." She looked at Carol with evident doubt. She said, "Do you know what a safety is?"

( 119 )

"No."

Maude showed her what a safety was; snapped it on and off. Carol shook her head slowly.

"Please, dear," Maude said. "Bill made me promise."

Carol dropped the little automatic into her handbag. It wasn't worth arguing about.

Floodlights were on above the driveway. She walked, on the grass, to the pink house. Just as she had fitted her key into the front door lock, the floodlights went off.

She went into the house and, for seconds, groped to find a light switch. Her fingers touched it and she flipped it up and three lamps lighted and the room was bright. She called, "Toby? Where are you, Toby?" and was not answered. She called again, momentarily uneasy. But he couldn't have got out; she had closed and locked all doors when she went out. "Toby? *Here*, Toby."

She went from room to room, turning on the lights in each. And Toby came out from under the bed in the bigger bedroom and stretched long, his forepaws clutching the bedroom carpet—wall to wall, as in a motel room—and his rear end high. He said "Yow. Ow—ooow!" He went past her at a trot, and went toward the kitchen.

Carol followed him, turning on lights—lights which she needed and Tobermory did not.

Toby looked at his empty dinner pan and up at her and said, "Yow-ow?"

"No," she said, "you've had your dinner. Don't you remember, cat?"

Cats like to be called "cat" in a friendly tone. It is reassuring. Not that they have any doubts about it, or lack of pride in their identity.

Carol pulled at the kitchen door which opened on the patio, testing. The door did not open. She turned the knob and the button clicked out, and she pulled again and the door opened. She stepped out into the patio. The moon had risen. It was a smaller moon than it had been the night before. In the moonlight she looked around the patio, a hedge-fenced oblong. No, not entirely fenced. At one end there was a gap in the hedge.

She went back into the lighted house and pressed on the button which locked the door.

She had left the small bedroom off the kitchen—the "maid's room"—to the last. She still carried her handbag and could feel its weight, which was greater than its usual weight. Almost surreptitiously, as if it were in some way an offense, she felt through the soft leather of the purse the hardness and the outline of the little automatic. Then she opened the door to the little room and groped for the switch and found it, and light sprang into the room.

The bed was smooth, as she had left it. The door to outside was closed; when she tugged at it without turning the knob it held against her. When she turned the knob the door opened on moonlight. She closed the door and pressed the button in the knob and the lock clicked. Locked. Which would not, of course, detain anyone to whom Millie's niece might have lent a key.

I was never like this before, Carol thought; never cautious in this worrying way before.

She went back into the kitchen and closed the door behind her. The door opened into the kitchen. I could, she thought, put a chair under the knob to wedge the door. But then she saw that, in the center of the knob, on the kitchen side, there was a locking button. She opened the door again. There was no keyhole in the other knob. There was only, in its center, a small round hole.

She closed the door and pressed the button in the knob. The lock clicked and when she pulled at the door without turning the knob, the door held. A key won't do anybody any good on this door, she thought. I'm as safe as locks can make me.

But she went to the hallway door which opened to the carport and made sure of it, and to the front door and pulled at the knob without turning it. As safe as locks can make me, Carol thought. But there is nothing to be safe against. No one means me harm or to make me fearful.

Toby had followed her from room to room, talking about things. She went through the house again, with Toby following, and turned out the lights she had put on. Her fingers were reluctant on the switches. When all lights were out except for those in the big bedroom, she went into the bedroom, hurrying from the darkness—from the moonlight which poured through windows, trickled through the jalousies.

Toby hurried after her. He jumped on the bed. She lifted him off it and said, "No, Toby. That was when we were on the road," and carried him to the door and put him out into the hallway and closed the door. Toby, his newly acquired license suspended, spoke in protest. She said, "No, Toby," through the door and undressed and got into the big bed. It was a comfortable bed, but she lay rigid in it.

I won't take them tonight, she thought. I'll just breathe deeply and wait, and sleep will come.

But Toby yowled outside the door and then began to scratch at it. She got up and found her sleeping capsules and took two of them and, hearing her move, Toby spoke more loudly than before and scratched more firmly.

She let her cat into the bedroom and closed them in together.

Toby jumped to the bed and turned himself a nest to curl in. She sat on the bed and was about to swing into it when she saw her handbag across the room on the table she had dropped it on. She got up again and crossed the room and took the little automatic out of the bag and put it in the drawer of the table by her bed. As safe as locks and a gun can make me, Carol thought—as safe from the uneasiness in my mind.

After a considerable time the rigidity went out of her body and, more slowly, out of her mind. After a time she slept.

Toby awakened her at a little after six with a soft paw on her lips and then with his purring. He had a resonant purr. She said, "We don't have to go any place today, cat," as soon as she remembered that they did not have to go out onto the highways again. But Toby spoke, rather sharply, and jumped off the bed and went to the door and looked up at the doorknob and made a remark and turned back to her and made another.

He would, she thought, sleepily, have to change his ways. But he is an adjustable cat. In a day or so—

She got out of bed and Toby led her to the kitchen and to his empty food plate. He told her to hurry. She put food into his plate and he too hurried, and she went back and got into bed again, closing her cat out. I won't get back to sleep, she thought. I'll just lie here for a few minutes and then get up and make myself coffee and—

Sunlight was coming in through the windows when she awakened, and it was almost ten o'clock. Briefly, she searched her mind for worries—for the morning uneasiness. She did not find it; she found that her mind was almost gay because the sun was shining and the air through the open window was warm. How silly I was last night, she thought. How fearful over nothing. And then, aloud, she laughed at herself. She had been so careful about the locks and had left a window open. Screened, to be sure. But screens are fragile— as fragile as last night's fears.

She put a light robe on and went, barefoot in warm air, to the kitchen. Toby, his breakfast finished, was curled in sleep on a living-room sofa. She made herself coffee and toast and, after a moment's hesitation, coddled herself two eggs. She ate at the kitchen table, and the food was fine.

She refilled her coffee cup and carried it, and cigarettes, into the living room and sat on the sofa beside Toby, who twitched the tip of his tail and purred absently and went back to sleep. The air came softly through the jalousies and the North was far away, and fog and fears as far. She lingered over coffee and three cigarettes. (I smoke too much nowadays. It doesn't matter this morning. This is a fine morning. I don't have to drive anywhere. It's sunny today, and I can go into the patio and sit in the sun.)

It was after eleven when she carried her cup back to the kitchen and put it, and the other dishes she had used, into the dishwasher. There was a box of detergent on top of the dishwasher and, under it, a note signed "M." "Put about two tsps. in thing in door." Maude is a thoughtful person, Carol thought. She spells things out. Carol pressed the button, and the dishwasher began to make noises, which were loud and, Carol hoped, suitable.

She unpacked and hung things in the closet. She went to the front door and opened it to see if it was really as warm as it seemed to be. It was. And across the little compound which held the three low, bright houses, Maude Hudson, in shorts and a halter, was kneeling beside a strip of flower bed and scratching soil with a cultivator. It's almost Thanksgiving, Carol thought, and still it's summer here.

She closed the door—and locked it—and put on a two-piece bathing suit and searched her toilet kit for the suntan lotion she must surely have brought with her. She said, "Damn!" when she found she had not. Without much hope, she opened the medicine cabinet in her bathroom. There was an unsqueezed tube of suntan lotion prominent on a shelf. Maude is really a woman who thinks of everything, Carol thought, in gratitude.

She transferred the contents of her leather handbag to a beachbag. She made sure about her door key. She spread lotion on arms and legs and shoulders and between bra and shorts. She went through the living room—saying "Have a nice nap, Toby"—and the kitchen and opened the door to the patio. And found the palm tree and the high hedges shaded the patio, which was the first anticlimax of this sunny morning.

The beach across the road? She lifted one of the beach chairs and it folded lightly in her hands. It weighs almost nothing, she thought, and made sure her key was in the beachbag and that the door was locked. She went through the gap in the hedge and walked, in sunshine, across grass, to the compound's gateway. She crossed the blacktop road and walked onto a bright beach and was alone on it, although here and there beach umbrellas stood in the white sand. She carried her chair near one of the umbrellas. She opened the chair and found that its back could be made to slant so the chair became a chaise. She put sun glasses on and lay in the chaise, and the sun beat on her.

After a time, she spread more suntan lotion on slim legs and arms and on the—How white I am!—area between bra and shorts.

Enough for now, she thought, after a longer time. Not too much to start with.

She looked across sand toward the ocean. Today it was a quiet ocean. She walked across white sand to the water and put her beachbag down beyond the water's reach and waded into the Atlantic, which was cold at first. When the water was deep she threw herself forward into it and swam away from land, and after a few strokes the water was no longer cold.

Fifty feet or so from the shoreline, she turned on her back and floated, in the sun. But the water glittered around her, and she swam back and walked onto the beach again. She toweled and put her sun glasses on and then looked up toward her waiting chair.

A man was standing by it—a man in slacks and a yellow polo shirt and sun glasses. He was looking across the sand toward her. He raised his right hand and tossed it in a relaxed salute.

She stopped. She took off her sun glasses so she could see more clearly. He was not an especially tall man; he was a lean man. He had a squarish face, deeply tanned. A wide smile broke the oblong of his face.

"Harmless, Mrs. Sanders," he said. "Quite harmless. A messenger from Maude."

She walked on across the sand toward the lean man—a youngish man, she thought. A man who looked as if he meant no harm. As she got nearer she saw a covered hamper on the sand in the umbrella's shade and, beside it, a folded beach chair like her own. The lean man kept on smiling as she approached him. He had taken off sun glasses and held them in his left hand.

He had brown hair, cut short. He had brown eyes. He said,

"Clay Arnold, Mrs. Sanders. Friend of Bill's and Maude's. Maude sent you some lunch." He pointed at the brown hamper. "Stopped by to return their lawn mower. Got turned into a Saint Bernard."

He smiled again. It was more grin than smile. He had a low, pleasant voice.

"You," he said, "have been taking a good deal of sun. I'll move you into the shade."

He swung her chair under the umbrella's shade. It had weighed little when she had carried it across the road. When he moved it it appeared to weigh nothing at all. She watched him. He moved her chair a little to one side and opened his own and put the hamper between them.

"Sit down in the shade," he told her. "Don't go on standing in the sun. You've had enough sun for now."

He instructed. But it did not feel like instruction.

"I don't burn badly," she said, but she went into the shade and sat on the chaise. She pulled the back up so that she was not lying on the chaise.

"Sun on you," he said. "Sun reflected from the water. Everybody burns, lady."

He did not sit on the other beach chair he had opened. He stood and looked down at her. He nodded his head, as if he were agreeing to something.

She said, "Clay Arnold? That's what you said? Names go out of my mind."

"I," he said, "am the sort who meets people half a dozen times at parties. Each time for the first time. Maude says there's enough for two. But should I then presume?"

There was something familiar in the shape of the last sentence. For a moment the familiarity escaped her. Then, to her own surprise, she said, "Yes, Mr. Prufrock."

"All this and T. S. Eliot too," he said, still standing, looking down at her. "All right, I'll stay for a drink."

He sat down and opened the lid of the hamper. He took a Thermos out of it and two plastic cups, and unscrewed the top of the Thermos. He watched her face. The smile

( 126 )

which was almost a grin flashed in his brown face. She did not know what had showed on her face. "It's all right," Clay Arnold said. "Made them myself. Maude's a dear and everything, but she's generous with vermouth. I'm stingy, myself. All right?"

She said, "Yes, Mr. Arnold," and then felt her own lips moving into a smile. "She is, rather," she said.

He put the plastic cups down on the smooth stand, twisting them so they would hold. He took a small cellophane envelope out of the hamper and, out of it, two slices of lemon peel. He poured into one of the cups and held lemon peel over it and twisted the peel. He said, "Drop it in?"

Carol said, "No, Mr. Arnold."

"After my own heart," Arnold said and filled the other cup and twisted peel over it. He put both twisted strips of peel back into the envelope. He said, "Discard no rubbish on the beach." He handed her one of the cups. Tiny sprinkles of the oil from the peel were disappearing in it. He raised his cup toward hers, but he did not say anything.

The martini was very cold and very dry and very good. He looked over his own cup at her and raised his eyebrows.

"Perfect," Carol said.

"If you drop the peel in," he said, "it bumps on your teeth."

She smiled again. She said, "Always. And then gets squishy."

"We share experiences," he said, and took a pack of cigarettes from a pocket of his slacks and shook one loose and held it toward her. It was the brand she smokes, which was coincidence. Unless Maude had said, "She likes martinis. She smokes Kents." It was quite possible Maude had. Maude was an observant and thoughtful person.

Clay Arnold lighted their cigarettes. He looked away from her toward the ocean. "It's quiet today," he said. "Most of the time it makes a racket. It's friendly today. Half the time it's in a rage. It's at peace today."

She turned a little so she could look at the Atlantic, which

( 127 )

was on its best behavior. She said, "Yes, Mr. Arnold. Quiet. A very relaxed ocean." She heard relaxation in her own voice.

"A peaceful place, Vero," he said. "Especially before the season starts. Late January it begins to fill up. Through March and into April. Then people begin to rush away."

"You sound," she said, "as if you live here the year around."

"Most of it," he said. "A few years ago I gave up rushing."

He drew deeply on his cigarette and ground it out in the sand, covering the butt with sand. He looked into his plastic cup as if there were something of importance in it. Then, with an unexpectedly quick movement, he raised the cup and tilted his head back.

"So," he said, "I've had my drink." He moved as if to stand up. But there was nothing decisive about the movement.

"You said there is enough lunch for two," Carol said.

"I did, didn't I?" Clay said, and lay back on the chaise. "I remember I said that. There is also another round."

The sun, the swim and the drink have relaxed me, Carol thought. He is pleasant, this friend of Maude's. He reads Eliot.

"They're very good martinis," Carol said, and held her glass out.

He put their plastic cups side by side in the sand and poured into them. He got fresh strips of lemon peel from the envelope and twisted them over the drinks and rubbed the twisted peel around the edges of the cups.

He handed hers back to her and again held his up toward it. This time he did say something. He said, "Peaceful days, Mrs. Sanders."

For a moment it seemed an odd way to phrase a toast. "Happy days." Or merely "Cheers." Or anything worn and familiar. The word "peaceful" apparently was a favorite word of his. She said, "Cheers," and drank. The martini was still cold, still good. He handed her another cigarette and lit it and lit one for himself.

"Because," he said, "I gather you need a peaceful time, Mrs. Sanders."

He answered a question she had not asked, had not even explicitly thought. He is a face-reader, she thought.

She said, "Need?"

He nodded his head.

"I suppose," Carol said, "Maude's been telling you about me? About—about what happened to Ben?"

"Yes," he said. "Oh, when it happened. When she flew up to New York."

"Did you know my husband too, Mr. Arnold?"

"Only of him," Clay Arnold said. "I see a bit of Maude and Bill. And of Felix and Vinnie, too. Your husband was almost never down here. The few times he was I didn't meet him. They talked about him."

"And about me," Carol said.

He said, "Of course. Maude got fond of you when she was in New York. Has been anxious about you since she came back. Didn't like your going through a bad time by yourself. You haven't any family of your own, apparently. Maude's a great one for families."

"No," Carol said. "No family. Not of my own."

Clay Arnold nodded his head. "Finish your drink," he said. "There aren't any more. We'll see what Maude's fixed up for us."

He did not say anything more about not sharing the food he had brought across the road to her.

What Maude had fixed for them was sandwiches—sandwiches of several kinds and in considerable numbers. It was by no means a lunch for one. It had never, Carol thought, been planned as a lunch for one. There were salads in little plastic bowls. A salad for each of them. There was a Thermos of coffee.

"Maude suggested beer," Clay said. "I thought you sounded more like a martini type."

"Sounded?"

"From what Maude said about you. Did I jump to the

( 129 )

wrong conclusion? Do sometimes, they tell me."

"No," Carol said. "I'm the martini type."

He smiled at her, she thought in approval.

They finished the sandwiches and the coffee. He lighted cigarettes for them and they smoked without talking. It was companionable, she thought. He's a pleasant man. He's probably in his middle thirties. She turned to look at him and found that he was looking at her. Little lines had formed between his eyebrows. He looks, she thought, as if he's making up his mind about me. Deciding about me.

She said, "Well, Mr. Arnold?"

"Oh," he said, "that you're a very pretty young woman. In spite of a touch of mayonnaise on your lower lip."

She wiped her lips with a paper napkin. She said, "Thank you, Mr. Arnold."

"Maude didn't describe you," he said. "Merely that you would be here. That you had come across alone, lugging a chair. That she hadn't seen anyone else on the beach."

"She keeps an eye on things," Carol said. It did not sound as appreciative as she had meant to sound. "She's a very thoughtful person, isn't she?"

"Yes," Arnold said. "That's probably the right word for Maudie." He began to put sandwich wrappings back into the hamper. "As a matter of fact, she called me up this morning to ask if I was through with the lawn mower. Because tomorrow is Lennie's day, or may be if he remembers it. She had the sandwiches ready when I got here, and the coffee hot for the Thermos. She let me make the martinis."

"Enough for two?"

He closed the hamper. He had been sitting on his heels. He stood up.

"Yes," he said. "Maude plans things. As you say, she's a very thoughtful person."

He folded his chair and stood, looking down at her, the light chair in one hand and the hamper in the other. He said, "Want me to carry the chair back for you?"

"No," she said. "I'll just sit a while longer. It was good of you to act as a Saint Bernard, Mr. Arnold."

( 130 )

His sudden smile was wide on his face. He said, "Woof, woof." He turned away and then turned back.

"Probably be seeing each other this evening," he said. "Bill and Felix and Vinnie are getting back this afternoon. Way Maudie plans it, we're all going over to the Grill for dinner. Me included."

She said, "Oh."

"It's quite a place, the Ocean Grill," he said. "Doubt if you've run into anything like it."

He walked off across the sand, carrying hamper and aluminum chair. He walked lightly across the sand, and across the road and through the gateway into the Sanders-Hudson compound.

She lighted a cigarette and lay in the shade and looked at the peaceful ocean. She thought of walking down the beach again and into the water, but she stayed on the chaise. She lowered the back of it so that she was lying on the chaise. She grew drowsy.

What I'll do, she thought, is to go back to the house and take a nap. She folded her chair and picked up it and her beachbag and walked across the sand. The sand tugged at her feet a little. The sand must have been packed more firmly where this Clay Arnold walked, she thought, vaguely.

# 9 ∽

She walked through the gap in the hedge around the patio. Sunlight was bright on the patio's grass; she would remember that. In early afternoon the patio was sunny. It would be a place in which to sun when she did not want to cross the road to the beach. She put the chaise down in the patio's deep grass and fumbled in her beachbag for her key. (Keys hide in deep bags.) She put the key in the lock of the kitchen door, and the brown face and blue eyes of Tobermory appeared, pressed against a pane of glass in the door. Toby made several remarks as she turned the key and pushed the door open. For a second, Toby, on hind legs and with forepaws against the door, went with the door.

He dropped to all fours and jumped toward the opening as it widened. Carol said, "No, Toby. *No!*" and blocked him with her foot. He tried to dodge the obstructing foot and again, with greater emphasis, she said, "*No!* No, Toby. *No!*"

"No" was a word which Tobermory understood entirely. It was not a word he liked in the least. He said so, at length, but submitted to the pushing foot, and she closed the door with her cat still in her house. "Tomorrow, maybe," she told her cat. "First you have to get used to the house. So you'll know to come back to it."

Toby said, "Yow-ow, ow yow," and turned his back on her and walked away. Then the telephone rang loudly and Toby ran to answer it. It had always been his conviction that all telephone calls were for him. He jumped on the arm of the living-room sofa and leaned toward the pale yellow telephone. Humans cannot be relied upon to find even the most obvious, and noisy, objects unless cats assist. Carol sat on the sofa and reached over Toby to the telephone and lifted the receiver and said, "Yes?"

"Carol? This is Maude. Did Arnold find you?"

"Yes," Carol said. "It was a wonderful lunch. We shared it. But you went to so much trouble. I could have—"

"You just got here," Maude told her. "You've had no time to get things in. It was the least I could do, dear. The very least."

"The very most," Carol told her. "Everything was perfect. You're spoiling me."

"Time somebody did," Maude said. "After everything and all those unpleasant things you thought—the things that happened to you driving down. Bill just called from the airport. They'll be along any minute. They—*wait* a minute. They just turned in. You'll hold on, dear?"

Carol said, "Of course," and heard Maude Hudson's heels clicking away on the tile floor. She heard, distantly, the opening of a door and then, "Bill!" Then, faintly, she could hear Maude's voice, but it was distant and she could not make out the words.

She's gone out to greet them, Carol thought. Her husband, whom I've never met, and Felix and Vinnie and—she heard heels clicking back on tile. Maude said, "Bill wants to say hello, dear. He's right here."

It was a man's voice then—a quick, hurrying voice. The man said, "This is Bill Hudson, Carol. Wanted to say hello. Tell you we're all glad you got here safely."

She said, "Hello, Bill. It's fine to be here."

It sounded flat in her ears.

"I thought you and Felix and Vinnie weren't getting here until tomorrow," she said.

"Got things squared away early," Wilbur Hudson said. "We—all right, Maudie." Then, "Maude wants to talk to you."

"Arnold tell you the plans for this evening?" Maude said. "About our all going over to the Grill for dinner?"

"Yes. Something. It sounds—"

"You'll love the Ocean Grill," Maude told her. "It's like nothing you've ever seen. And the food's wonderful."

"It sounds—" Carol said again, but was not waited for.

"Here for drinks," Maude said. "About six. We'll all go over in Felix's car. All right, dear?"

"Fine," Carol said. "It sounds fine, Maude. You're all—all being too good to me."

"We're your family now," Maude said. "We love having you here. Sixish, then?"

"Sixish," Carol said, and heard the click as Maude hung up and put her own receiver back in its cradle.

Toby turned on the arm of the sofa so he faced her. He told her, with emphasis, that it was past time for his lunch. He jumped down and showed her the way to the kitchen, turning his head around at intervals to see if she had got the point.

She went after him and fed him and found that he had used his toilet pan, which meant that he had accepted his new house.

Toby went at his food with the eagerness of a starving cat. Carol picked up his toilet pan and looked around and thought, Probably the trash can is out in the patio. But I don't remember—

She opened the door to the patio, with a wary ear toward Toby and the sound of his tongue rasping on aluminum and his teeth crunching Friskies.

There was no trash can visible in the patio. Maude must have told me where it is, Carol thought. And I didn't listen. It must—

She looked around the kitchen. Near the door which opened to the patio there was a cupboard which jutted out into the room. It had two doors, and she opened one.

Inside were two trash cans, their lids on firmly. There was also a vacuum cleaner and, somewhat unexpectedly, a lawn mower and a rake. She tugged the top from one of the cans.

It was half full of newspapers and discarded cleaning rags. There were two punctured and empty beer cans and an empty bottle of Windex.

She poured the contents of Toby's toilet pan into the trash can and put the lid back on it and closed the cupboard and filled the pan with Klean Kitty, wishing—as she always did—that so useful a material had a less kittenish name. Toby looked up from his lunch to see that she was doing what she should do. He pursued the final tiny ball of Friskies around his pan and caught it and crunched it between strong, white teeth.

Carol made sure that all the doors were locked, including that which opened to the maid's room in which somebody, but apparently not a maid, had slept two nights before. She went across the kitchen and then went back and opened the door to the maid's room. The room was empty, the knob button of the outer door pushed in to the locking position and the single bed smooth as she had left it. She closed the door and, once again, made sure of the lock—I'm getting an obsession about locked doors, she thought, and shook her head at herself.

She went to her bedroom and shut Toby out of it, an action on which he commented unfavorably, and stripped off swimming trunks and halter and stretched on the bed. She pulled a sheet over her and, almost at once, slept. She slept without dreams.

It was after five when she wakened. She stretched and kicked the sheet off and felt fine. Why, she thought, my cold's gone; finally it's all gone. Just a few hours in the sun and it's all gone. Toby, hearing her movements, spoke from behind the closed door, but he did not speak in his aggrieved tone. He spoke softly, in friendship, which is a concession, and a difficult one, for a Siamese cat. She said, "After a while, Toby. And you just had lunch."

Toby answered, still without animus, and she swung out of bed. She ran the shower warm at first, then cold. It was not especially cold. She looked at the dresses she had brought with her and pulled off its hanger one she had bought at

Saks the week before she left New York. It was an orange and white print and the saleswoman had insisted that the skirt was not too short. "Not with legs like yours, dear," the saleswoman had told her. "It's *you*, dear."

She put a face on, with care. She put on the orange and white sleeveless print and looked at herself in the full-length mirror in the bathroom door and thought, Perhaps it is me, after all. It is short, of course. But they were all short. A year ago they were going to get longer, but they never have. She put on white shoes. It had been months since she had worn white shoes. She thought, My great-grandmother always wore black after her husband died. She even, grandmother used to tell me, wore a black bonnet with something—oh, yes, with little dangles of something they called "jet."

Carol got a lightweight white jacket from a hanger and slipped it on and thought, I look like summer. I hope it's all right here to look like summer.

Toby met her at the door and rubbed against her legs, purring loudly. Then he showed her the way to the kitchen. Again she told him he had just had lunch; that six in the evening was not yet time for his dinner. He had other views and expressed them loudly. "You'll wake the neighbors," she told him, but she followed him to the kitchen and dropped Little Friskies into his pan. They bounced in it and Toby bounced after them.

She went out the front door and made sure it was locked behind her, and that the key was in her handbag. But I didn't go around and check the other doors, she thought. I'm all right again. She walked across to Maude's house on the driveway gravel. Tall grass a little in need of cutting can stain white shoes.

There was a big black Continental standing in front of the Hudsons' house. The light from the flood lamp glittered from the Continental's immaculate body. She went around the big car and Maude Hudson, who was wearing a short white sheath, opened the door and said, "Carol, dear, you look *lovely*. And so *rested*. Already it's showing."

"I feel fine," Carol said. "It was fine on the beach."

She followed Maude into the big living room. Soft air still came through the partly opened jalousies. The room glowed with the light from low lamps. Two men stood up. Both wore white jackets and dark slacks.

One of them was a slight man with black hair and almost black eyes. He moved quickly toward her, with a hand out. He said, "I'm Bill, Carol. Bill Hudson." He spoke very quickly, hurrying his words, as he had on the telephone.

The other man was much taller and he was also lean. He, too, held out a hand to her—it was a strong, browned hand. He said, "She knows your last name, Bill. I'm your brother-in-law, Carol. Felix. Welcome to your family."

He was as tall as his brother had been; had the blue eyes of his brother. He was younger; he was not as heavy as Ben had been. Looking up at him, saying something meaningless to him but letting a smile supply meaning, Carol thought, He doesn't really look much like Ben. I was afraid he might. Brothers do, sometimes, look alike.

"And," Maude said, "this is Vinnie, dear."

Vinnie was pretty and blond and, Carol thought, about my age. Her blond hair fell to her shoulders; fell in soft curls. She had blue eyes and had used a good deal of eye shadow. She used silver polish on her fingernails. She held a hand up to Carol, the nails glittering in the light, and said, "Darling. I'm so glad finally."

"So am I," Carol said, taking the offered hand.

"And now," Bill Hudson said, speaking as if a considerable time had elapsed, "what can I get you?"

They all had short, squat glasses, with, Carol supposed, Scotch on the rocks.

"I told you, Bill," Maude said. "She drinks martinis."

"It doesn't matter," Carol said. "Whatever the rest—"

"Nonsense," Maude said. "Of course it matters, dear."

"Sure does," Bill said, and went—moving fast, as if he were late for something—down the room to a table with bottles and glasses on it and an ice container. At the bar

( 137 )

table he turned and said, "Want an olive in it? There's lemon peel if you'd rather. And on the rocks or straight up?"

"Lemon peel," Carol said down the room. "And up, if it's all the same."

She thought of adding, "Very little vermouth, please," but decided against it. Anyway, with hands, Bill Hudson was already pouring from bottle onto ice in a shaker. He did not measure; he was, Carol saw with slight foreboding, one of those who mix by splash.

"Sit right there," Maude told her and pointed to a chair, and Carol sat right there. Hudson hurried up the room with a stemmed glass on a little tray and put it down on a table beside her chair. She said "Thank you" to the hurrying man, who smiled at her and nodded quickly.

"To all of us," Felix Sanders said and raised his glass. "To the family."

They drank to that. The martini, measured by splash or not, was cold and good enough. A bit too much vermouth, but good enough. Not as clean and tart as the ones Clay Arnold had brought to her on the beach, but good enough. Apparently Clay Arnold had found something else to do. Or, perhaps, was going to join them at this restaurant.

"Did you have a good trip down?" Felix asked her and she said, "Oh, a fine trip," and then, to round it off, added his name to the phrase. Then she said, "It's a long drive down. I was glad to get here."

"She didn't have, really," Maude said. "Did you, dear? All sorts of annoying things."

"Usually are," Felix said. He spoke slowly, relaxation in his voice. "Traffic the way it is nowadays."

"The first day," Maude said, "she got the idea—"

A car's engine snorted outside and stopped. It interrupted Maude's sentence, which was, Carol thought, a good sentence to be interrupted. I shouldn't have told her all those niggling things, Carol thought. My mind was full of them yesterday. It is empty of them now. I hope she doesn't—

It was Bill Hudson who went to the door. He almost ran

to the door and pulled it open with a kind of abruptness. He said, "Hi, Clay," and held the door open, and Clay Arnold came into the room. He, like the other men, wore a white jacket and dark slacks. He wore a pale blue shirt and a darker blue necktie. The smile which was almost a grin slit his tanned face. He said, "Hi, everybody," and then, "Sorry I'm late."

Carol looked, involuntarily, at the watch on her wrist. It was six-thirty. Six-thirty is not really late for a time set at "sixish."

"Had a couple of telephone calls," Clay said. "Held me up longer than I thought they would."

"It's all right, dear," Maude Hudson said. "Perfectly all right. The reservation isn't until seven."

Bill Hudson said, "The usual? Or you want to make it yourself?"

"I'll make it," Clay said and looked at Carol. "Woof woof?"

"Not yet," Carol said, and felt that her own smile up to him was a little like a grin.

Clay walked what she felt was a familiar way down the room to the table which was a bar. He put ice in a shaker and measured gin onto it. He added vermouth. He came back carrying a stemmed glass by its stem between long brown fingers. He sat in a chair next Carol's and lifted his glass toward her and said, as he had on the beach, "Peaceful days." He sipped from his glass. He said, "Today was, Mrs. Sanders?"

She raised her own glass and nodded over it. She said, "Very." Maude said, "You're supposed to call her Carol. She's family." Clay Arnold raised his eyebrows for an instant and then said, "Carol?" He had, she thought, a good voice. A voice with texture in it.

"Of course," she said.

"No more—incidents?"

"A man brought me lunch," she said. "A very good lunch." She smiled across the room at Maude and then, when what he had said caught up in her mind, the smile faded. "More" incidents. Then Maude, while she finished with sandwiches, while he made martinis and poured them into a Thermos, had told him what she had been told of the little things, the little troubling things, which had happened between New York and Vero. Why?

"Yes," Clay said, and she realized he had been watching her face while she smiled toward Maude and while the smile faded away. "Yes. Maudie is a sieve." He looked at Maude and smiled at her and said, "Aren't you, dear?"

"I was only telling you about her," Maude said. "About the things which happened to her on the way down. So that— oh, if she seemed a little keyed up, you'd understand."

"She didn't," Clay Arnold said. "A very quiet, relaxed lady."

"I don't," Vinnie Sanders said, "have any idea what you're all talking about."

Vinnie had a voice—a light, fluting voice—which seemed to Carol to go with her long, softly curled blond hair.

"It's nothing," Carol said. "Nothing that matters at all."

But a little of the uneasiness, some of the itching fears, crept back into her mind. Abruptly, she finished her drink and Clay Arnold, watching her, said, "Woof-woof?"

She shook her head and put the glass down on the table and fingered a pack of cigarettes out of her purse and a cigarette from the pack. She turned to the flame of the lighter which Clay held out to her. He nodded his head at her, but she did not know why. She felt that she was supposed to know; that she was supposed to read his face, as on the beach he had seemed to read hers. She moved her lips into a smile but knew it was a smile which ended with the movement of her lips.

"I don't want to hurry anybody," Maude said, and looked around at the others, and at still partly filled glasses. "But you all know how they are at the Grill."

Apparently all did know how "they" were at the Grill, which Carol assumed was insistent on punctuality. Glasses were emptied, Bill Hudson's in a quick gulp. Maude stood up and said, "The facilities?" Nobody wanted the use of facilities. Maude said, "Then?" and Felix said, "We'll all fit in our car."

"Or," Clay Arnold said, "Carol can come with me."

"She'll get blown," Vinnie said, and stood—Her dress is even shorter than mine, Carol thought; her legs aren't anything special—and smoothed long blond hair with both hands.

"Do you mind getting blown?" Arnold said, and smiled down at Carol. "There isn't any top on the thing. But it's only a few blocks and it's a quiet night."

"No," she said. "I don't mind getting blown."

The "thing" was a dark green Mercedes, very low to the ground, its dash crowded with dials. But it was only a few blocks, back the way she had come the evening before. Clay did not drive fast, although the little car seemed to be built for speed. After a short distance, he waved his left arm, pointing, and said, "You play golf? That's the course. It's an all-right course."

"No," she said. "I used to play tennis. Never golf."

"Lot of walking in golf," Arnold said. "Supposed to be very relaxing."

They passed shops, the Continental coming behind them. The Mercedes turned right and loitered toward the ocean; it nudged between white lines diagonal to the curb. The Continental went past them. Then it, too, found a parking place.

They walked, up the sidewalk's slope, toward the Atlantic, and surf sound grew as they neared the ocean. At the big Continental they joined the others and walked on toward an electric sign which said, "OCEAN GRILL." Felix Sanders reached a long arm out around his wife and pulled a door open, and held it open for the others. They went into a small lobby, in which there were already half a dozen people waiting beside a large desk. A man in a dark suit came up two steps beyond the half-dozen and said, "All ready now," and the six followed him down the steps.

The woman behind the desk said, "Are you all togeth—oh, good evening, Mrs. Hudson. Your table's all ready."

She stood up and came around the desk, and Carol looked down into the restaurant. Unconsciously, she gasped slightly.

"Yes," Arnold said, beside her. "It's quite a place."

It was a very big place, stretching out below the platform lobby. There was a feeling of great weight about the place, and Carol realized that that was because all the many chairs and tables were of dark wood. Most of the chairs had high wooden backs. At the bottom of the two steps and a little to one side there was an enormous round table—a table which, she guessed, must be sixteen feet in diameter. It was set for many people, but nobody sat at it. Above the round table there was a black iron wheel, held up by chains from ceiling girders of heavy, dark wood, and little light bulbs were bright around the great iron circle. Inside the wheel there was a steeple of iron rods which bent together to a point just below the ceiling.

"They say," Arnold said, a step behind her on the stairs, "that it's all one piece of wood—one slice from a redwood tree."

The big table was the only empty table. The other heavy, polished tables through the stretching room had people sitting at them—tables for four and six and, beside thick pillars, tables for two. There were men in white dinner jackets and in plaid jackets and green jackets; a good many of the women wore mink stoles. There was conversation between the tables, and the fluttering of hands from table to table.

"Animated," Arnold said. "Everybody comes here. At five-thirty, most evenings, they begin to line up. From early November until the first of April. The same people, pretty much the same people, every year. A colony."

They followed the Hudsons and the Sanderses, who followed the woman with coiffed white hair, who wore a black dress with white edging collar and short sleeves, across the big room. They stopped to let Negro boys carry enormous trays between tables and put them down on stands; they side-stepped waitresses in white uniforms and green uniforms who darted between tables and put plates down

( 142 )

in front of people and took plates away from in front of people. The waitresses in green uniforms carried, on the tips of fingers, small trays with filled glasses on them and empty glasses on them. "So sorry," waitresses said when, momentarily, they blocked progress. *"So sorry!"*

They went, after the others, toward a wall which was almost all glass jalousies. Beyond it, lights shone down on the ocean and the ocean broke in frothy white under the lights. Surf sound rushed in at them through the partly opened jalousies. The ocean seemed to be snatching at the building. The ocean could not quite reach what it snatched at.

An iron railing separated from the rest of the enormous restaurant a section closest to the sea. Near the railing, there were tables for four and for six; along the jalousied wall were tables for two, with small lamps on them. They followed the others down one step to this slightly lower level, and to the right and a table set for six and with a "Reserved" sign on it. "Sit there," Maude told Carol, and pointed. "So you can see the water."

Carol sat where she could see the water, and Clay Arnold went behind her chair and sat in the one next it. They circled the table; a waitress in green said, above the roar of the water—but the ears grew accustomed to the surf's beating—"Cocktails before dinner?" and they ordered cocktails. A waitress in white brought them large menus—gigantic menus. "Lobster Stuffed with Crab Meat." "Broiled Pompano (in season)" "Our Specialty: Roast Prime Ribs of Beef!" (The beef rated an exclamation point.)

"Everything is good here," Maude assured the others.

A waitress—this one in blue—wheeled a cart to the table and, as they were pointed out to her, forked pickles and olives and strips of celery onto small plates and spooned on other relishes, some of which baffled Carol Sanders; at most of which she shook her head and said, "No, thank you." The waitress in green brought their drinks on a tray and remembered which drink went in front of each. They sipped and talked.

"How was it on the Coast?" Arnold asked Felix Sanders and was told, by him and by Vinnie and by Bill Hudson, that things had been fine on the Coast, if a little hectic, and that it was good—Vinnie said "divine"—to get back. "To civilization," Felix said.

They finished drinks. Bill Hudson, with a quick, abrupt movement, summoned the waitress in a green uniform and waved his hand in a circle toward all the glasses. But Carol put her hand over hers and shook her head at the waitress. "Woof-woof?" Arnold said, into her right ear. "I'm woofed for now," Carol said.

"You must, dear," Maude said across the table. "It's a celebration. Your being here at last.

It was nothing to make a point of. Carol raised her shoulders in acceptance and nodded to the waitress.

"Only," Maude said, "we'd probably better decide what we want to eat. They cook everything to order, you know."

The waitress in white hovered and they ordered. Carol ordered pompano, and Arnold said, "You'll like it. About the best fish around, except, sometimes, yellowtail." But he ordered roast beef, if they had it rare. "However you want it, sir."

There was a wait of some little time, presumably for pompano—and the lobster stuffed with crab meat which Vinnie had ordered—and Carol was glad she had the extra martini to swish in her glass and to sip at. (Without a drink to swish, one merely waits vacantly for food.) And, with this second—no, third!—drink, the tightness which had pinched at her mind, briefly, at the Hudsons' house relaxed again.

The pompano was delicious. The waitress brought three small loaves of bread and sliced them on a board, and the bread was homemade—just made and warm from the oven. The butter tasted, and in its soft pats looked, as if it had come from a private churn.

Carol finished her fish, nibbled at excellent salad, and looked out at the water, as she had been told to do. The water crested white in the restaurant's floodlights. This is a wonderful place to be, she thought. For all the ocean's uneasiness, its insistence, this is a restful place.

People got up from the tables for two between her and the tossing water, and other people, led by the woman with coiffed white hair or by the man in the dark suit, replaced them. Two men, one of them in a bright red jacket, took one of the vacated tables, and they looked, she thought, as if they had been waiting a long time for a free table and had been waiting at the bar. A slender young couple left a table and it was cleared, and a heavy, not young, couple took it. The woman wore a mink stole, the man a turtleneck sports shirt. He was not, Carol thought idly, constructed for a turtleneck shirt.

A table to her right as she looked at the ocean through the jalousies was cleared and set again, and the woman with white hair led a man to it. The man wore a gray suit. He sat so that, diagonally, he faced toward Carol.

She drew in her breath in a quick, almost choking gasp, and Clay Arnold turned in his chair and looked at her. He said, "All right, lady?"

She did not answer him, nor did she look at him. She pushed her chair back and stood up, her napkin wadded in her hand. She dropped her napkin on her chair and went behind Clay and around the table, and the others watched her. She could feel them watching her.

She went to the table where the man in the gray suit sat and he stood up and she said, "You're Detective Bronson." She did not make a question of it. Bronson nodded his head. He said, "Yes, Mrs. Sanders."

"You caught up with me," she said.

Bronson said, in his quiet voice—a voice the surf sound almost drowned—"Caught up with you?"

"Followed me down here," she said. "Did things to frighten me. Why?"

"I don't know what you mean," Bronson said. "I didn't follow you. I'm on my way—"

"In a car with red splotches on a fender," Carol said. "You

( 145 )

turned on the lights of my car so the battery would run down. To make me—to make me what? Break down? To wear me down. Was that it? Is that the way policemen like you do things?"

"I don't know what you're talking about, Mrs. Sanders. Why would I—why would any policeman—do that? We don't, you know."

"Let people think they're all right," she said, and spoke very quickly. "That they're not suspected of anything. But —follow them. Let them know they're being followed. Until they are so shaken they'll—they'll admit anything. Is that the way it's done? What's it called, Mr. Bronson? Putting them on a string? Or giving them enough rope? Am I supposed to confess to something? Break down and tell you, yes, I pushed my husband out of a tenth-floor window? Is that what you want?"

He shook his head. He shook it slowly, and his shoulders became part of the motion. For some seconds he did not say anything, but merely slowly shook his head.

"I don't know what's the matter with you," he said finally, and spoke as slowly as he had moved his head. "I never thought anything like that. Nobody did. I think your husband was facing a serious operation and decided he couldn't face it. I think that the tumor growing in his brain had affected his mind. I haven't what you call caught up with you, Mrs. Sanders. There's no reason I should, is there?"

"As soon as I came to this table you knew who I was," she said. "It was a long time ago you came to the apartment to ask me questions. You must go to dozens of places— hundreds of places—and ask people questions. Yet you knew me right away. Before I came here, while I was at the other table, you knew who I was. Isn't that right?"

"Yes," he said. "I remember faces. It's part of my trade to remember faces. I didn't follow you here. I didn't know you'd be here."

"You know I was coming to Vero," she said. "I told you I might. I called up your office to tell you I had decided I would come here. You weren't there, but I left a message with someone else."

"Yes," he said. "I got the message. They called me about it. Just before I left New York—the night before. They told you, didn't they, that I was on leave?"

"All right," she said. "They told me that. Detective somebody told me that. But it wasn't true, was it? You waited outside my apartment in a big car, didn't you? Followed me down the turnpike, making sure I knew you were following me. That's the way it really was, isn't it?"

Again he shook his head slowly. Then he said, "When did you leave New York, Mrs. Sanders? Imagine somebody was following you?"

"Monday," she said. "Early Monday morning. It was foggy."

"Yes," he said. "It was foggy Monday morning. And I was in Felony Court, giving evidence. I left New York Tuesday. Quite early Tuesday. I drive a Volks, Mrs. Sanders. Not what you call a big car. I got here this afternoon—three or four hours ago. I checked into a motel."

He spoke slowly, as if he were afraid she would not follow his words.

"And just happened to come here for dinner." She heard skepticism, which was close to contempt, in her own voice.

"No," he said. "I was here two years ago. And two years before that. I save up my time off, Mrs. Sanders. I've enough seniority to manage that. I save up my money. I go down to Marathon—it's one of the keys, Mrs. Sanders. I go fishing. For four or five days I go fishing. Find some other guy to share the charter of a boat. Then I drive back and go back to work."

"Catching people instead of fish," she said. "Am I supposed to believe this? That you—you just happen to be here when I'm here? That it's just a coincidence?"

"I can't tell you what to believe," he said, and still spoke slowly. "It happens to be the way I tell you it is. If somebody followed you on the way down—" He broke off and

( 147 )

again shook his head. This time it seemed to her that his eyes narrowed. He said, "What makes you think somebody followed you, Mrs. Sanders? There are always cars behind you on the road. Sometimes it's the same car for miles."

"You were driving a big black car," she said. "I don't know what kind of car. There were streaks of red on its right front fender." She stopped speaking, because it was no use going on. But then she said, "You think I imagined it? Or just made it up? Why would I make it up—it and the other things that happened?"

"Other things?"

"You must think I'm a fool," she said. "Or—do you think I'm crazy? You know what other things."

"No," he said. "I don't know about other things. Any other things. I've no way of knowing whether you made things up in your own mind. You were under a strain those times I saw you in New York. People get odd quirks when they're under strain. I'm not saying you made up whatever those other things were. I don't think you're crazy."

"You think I—flew apart," she said, and now her voice was dull—so dull the sound of the surf almost swept over it. "Pushed my husband out of a window. Or—or do you think I didn't fly apart? Pushed him out so—I don't know. So I would inherit his money? Or because I hated him. Or—"

A bar waitress brought a tall drink and put it down on the table in front of which Bronson stood. He said, "Thank you," and then he sat down. He put fingers around the tall glass. But he looked up at her.

"No," he said, and again spoke slowly in a lower voice than he had used before. "I don't think you pushed Mr. Sanders out the window. I didn't follow you down here. And now I want to have a drink and something to eat and drive back to my motel—in the Volkswagen I drove here in, Mrs. Sanders—and sleep and get up early in the morning and drive down to Marathon." He took a swallow from his glass.

"And fish," Detective Bronson said. "Last year I got a sail. Maybe this year I'll get another." He drank again. "And if I do I'll let it go," he said. "Perhaps hoist it aboard, if it looks

( 148 )

like a big one, and weigh it and then let it go. Let it swim away."

He quit looking at her. He turned in his chair and beckoned a waitress.

She turned and walked back to the round table. She felt the rigidity of the muscles of her face. She felt disbelief rigid in her mind.

I'll say it was just a man I used to know, she thought, around the core of rigidity in her mind. I'll tell them he's a man who used to work at the office. I must smile and tell them he's only a man who used to work in the same office.

He's wearing a revolver in a holster under his jacket, she thought. If I'd asked him that he'd probably have told me he's going to shoot sailfish.

# 10 ☙

She tried to relax the muscles of her face as she walked back to the table; tried to look like a woman who had seen a chance acquaintance of long ago and gone to say hello to him. She tried to adjust her lips to a casual smile, as the others looked up at her. She went behind Clay Arnold. She started to sit down, forgetting—having never really known—that she dropped her wadded napkin on the chair after she had seen Bronson.

Arnold's right hand was quick. It whisked the napkin from the chair and put it on the table by her plate. He looked at her, his eyes narrowed a little, a tiny line between his eyebrows.

"A man I used to know," she said; said in answer to the waiting expression on the faces of the others. "He used to work at Byrant and Washburn. Where I work."

The Hudsons, Felix and Vinnie Sanders, nodded their heads to show they understood. Clay did not nod his head; he continued to look at her, and the little line remained between his eyebrows.

"A man named Jenkins," she said. "Claude Jenkins. He was assistant advertising manager when I first went there. I never knew him well."

Add detail; detail builds up a lie.

"You should have brought him over," Maude said. She turned in her chair and smiled toward Detective Bronson.

( 150 )

But Bronson was looking out of the window beside him at the tossing, white-capped water. Maude turned back. "We'd love to meet friends of yours, dear," she told Carol across the table.

"Not a friend really," Carol said, and her voice sounded dull, distant, in her own ears. "Just a man I used to know."

"Some dessert now?" their waitress asked them. "Ice cream? Our own homemade pie?"

I hope they don't, Carol thought. I want to get away from here. I want to get where this man in the gray suit can't look at me.

"The chocolate cream pie looks very good," the waitress told them.

No, Carol thought. *Please no. I want to get away from here.* She could feel that Clay Arnold, although he was looking at his menu, was, somehow, also looking at her; was thinking about her.

Vinnie Sanders would try the pie. And Maude thought she would have chocolate ice cream. The waitress looked at Carol. "Just coffee, please," Carol said, and felt her voice still dull, muted. Felix and Bill Hudson ordered, and the waitress waited for Clay Arnold, who still was looking at the menu. He put the menu down. "Just coffee for me," he said.

Desserts came and coffee came—hot and fragrant coffee. Carol was conscious only of its heat; of its heat on tongue and throat. She wanted to turn her head and look at Bronson, sitting by himself, sipping from his tall drink. She would not let herself look at him.

Beside her, Clay Arnold drank his coffee rapidly, as if it were not too hot to swallow rapidly. He put his cup down and the waitress held a glass container toward him. She said, "Shall I heat it up for you, sir?"

"No," Arnold said. "Thanks, but no." Then he turned and looked at Carol, who was looking away at the cresting water. But she felt that he was looking at her and turned and moved her lips into the smile which was not a smile. He did not smile back at her, but he nodded his head briefly, as if he had decided something.

( 151 )

"I think," he said, "the others will excuse us if I take you home, lady. It was a long drive down. Probably you're tireder than you realize. Takes a while to bounce back after driving hundreds of miles." He still did not smile and his eyes, still a little narrowed, seemed to her oddly intent. "Anyway," he said, "it always does me."

"Thought we'd all go back to the house for a night—" Bill Hudson said, but Maude shook her head at him and did not let him finish. She said, "No, dear. Clay's right. She *is* tired. She ought to be home in bed. These long trips—" She shook her head in sympathy for one who had made so long a trip.

"Tell you what," Clay Arnold said, and pushed his chair back and began to stand up. "The rest of you just take your time and I'll drive Carol home." He looked down at Carol Sanders. "All right with you, lady?" he asked her, and put a hand on the back of her chair.

"Yes," she said, and he pulled the chair back. She said, "It's been a lovely party. I don't like to be the one to break it up. But I *am* tired. Probably you're right, Maude. Probably I'd better go back to the house and get a long night's sleep."

She stood up and the other men stood. "It's been so good to meet all of you," Carol said, and felt the words were vague words, and meaningless.

"Lady," Clay Arnold said, "you're asleep on your feet." He touched her shoulder gently and she smiled once more at the others, and the smile was what it had been before. She walked between heavy tables, some of them empty. Clay Arnold walked behind her. Now nobody was waiting in front of the big desk in the little lobby. The woman with coiffed white hair looked up from dinner checks she was sorting and hoped they had enjoyed their dinners. "Very much," Carol said. "Everything was delicious."

"Come and see us again," the white-haired woman said, and went back to shuffling papers.

Clay moved forward to walk beside her and they went out into still, just cool, air. They walked down the sloping sidewalk to the topless green Mercedes and neither of them said anything. The leather seat of the car was a little damp as she sat on it. Clay ran a hand over his own bucket seat. He brushed his hand with the other. "Could be we'll get fog by morning," he said. "Do sometimes this time of year." He turned the ignition key and the motor jumped to life. He turned to Carol. He said, "You're not cold, are you?"

She said, "No, I'm not cold."

He backed the car out of its slot and turned it and drove, slowly, to the foot of the sloping roadway. He stopped and turned left on Ocean Drive. Neither of them said anything as the car, its eagerness curbed, carried them the few blocks to the pillared gateway and into the compound. He drove up to her pink house and stopped the car and flicked the lights off. He got out of the low car and walked around it and opened the door on her side and held a hand down to her. She took the narrow, hard hand, and he pulled her gently up from the bucket seat.

He walked beside her to the door of the house, and she opened her handbag and it seemed uncertain in her hands. He held it up for her while she groped her key out of it. He took the key from her and turned it in the lock. He reached inside to a switch and lights went on in the big room, so like the big room of Maude Hudson's house. Then he stepped back and she went into the house. He went after her, as if he were supposed to go in with her.

She said, "Toby?" which was a reflex. When she went into any place she shared with her cat she always spoke his name. He answered her from her bedroom and then came out of it. At the door from hall to living room he stopped and look at the two of them. Sometimes when people he did not know were with her he left and, without hurrying, without losing his dignity, went under something convenient. This time he did not. He looked them over. He came to rub against her legs. Then, after looking up again at Clay Arnold, he rubbed himself against Arnold's legs. He purred. He had a very resonant purr.

He spoke to Carol, then, and went out toward the kitchen.

( 153 )

"He's a handsome cat," Clay said. "Good head. Good lines. He—"

"You knew I wanted to leave," Carol said. "How did you know that? Was I so—so obvious?"

"No," he said. "You weren't obvious. I just—call it guessed you wanted to get away."

"Do you read faces? she asked him. "The way some people read palms?"

"I look at people. Part of my—"

He shook his head and did not go on. She waited a moment, and he shook his head again. She said, "There isn't anything to drink except—I brought some mixed martinis down with me. Mixed them myself. But—"

She shrugged slim shoulders under the summer dress; shrugged away the thought of a martini after dinner.

"Bill was going to give us nightcaps," she said. "They ought to be back very soon. Perhaps they're back already."

"I don't need a drink," Clay Arnold said. "Was it because of that man at the restaurant? The old acquaintance of yours? The man named Jenkins?"

"I was just tired," she said. "It—as Maude said, it's a long drive down. I was—was more tired out than I'd realized. It hadn't anything to do with Mr. Jenkins."

It's the wrong way to put it, she thought. I should have called him by his given name. Not called him "mister." What did I tell them his given name was?

They were still standing near the center of the big room. He reached out and touched her arm as he had at the restaurant, and again it was a guiding touch. She went to the wide sofa and sat down on it and he stood for a moment, looking down at her. Then he took two long, light strides across the room and sat beside her.

Tobermory came in from the kitchen and sat on the floor in front of them and looked up at them. He said, "Yow?" as a question. She said, "Yes, Toby. All right, Toby," and he jumped to the sofa between them. He walked across Clay Arnold and sat beside him and the cat's purr was loud. Arnold's fingertips moved gently behind Toby's pointed, black-brown ears. Arnold told him he was a good cat, and Toby stretched so that more of his long body was available to a caressing hand.

"A purebred," Arnold said, stroking Toby. "A good one, at a guess. A valuable one? I mean, valuable enough to steal?"

"No," she said. "He's not a breeding cat now. Just—my cat." She had been looking over Clay, watching his long fingers stroking her cat. She looked into Clay Arnold's face. She said, "Steal?" and then, after a moment, "Why did you say that?"

"No reason," he said. "Just idle—" But he stopped when she shook her head at him. For some seconds she merely continued to look at him.

"No," she said. "Maude told you he disappeared from my room the other night. Because somebody had taken the screen off the window. But I thought somebody had stolen him. Maude told you that, didn't she? That's why you asked whether Toby's a valuable cat. Valuable in money. Isn't that it?"

"Yes," Arnold said. "I suppose that's it."

"Told you that? And the other things that happened?"

"Yes."

"Why would she tell you about it? It isn't any concern of yours. What did she say? 'My poor sister-in-law's imagining things'? That she's—how would Maude put it? Off her rocker? Bats? Or, just plain crazy."

"She didn't say any of those things. I don't know why she told me about these things that happened to you on the way down."

"That I imagine happened. Things that happened only in my mind. Because—what's the proper word for it, Mr. Arnold? Do you know the proper word? Because I'm paranoid? Is that it?"

Arnold shook his head. His fingers continued to stroke Toby, and Toby's purring was deep. The tip of Toby's long black-brown tail twitched.

"No," Arnold said. "Maude didn't say, didn't imply, these things hadn't happened. I don't know why she told me

( 155 )

about them." He looked down at the cat he was stroking. "Don't really know, Carol."

"About somebody in the next room playing a tune that was a favorite of mine and of Ben's? About the man who telephoned me, but asked for somebody else? A man whose voice was Ben's voice?"

"No," he said. "She didn't tell me those things. That somebody followed you on the Jersey Turnpike, yes. That one morning your battery was almost down because, you thought, somebody had turned the lights on to run it down. Not anything about somebody's telephoning you. A man whose voice sounded to you like that of your husband. Did you tell her those things?"

"I don't know," Carol said. "I don't remember what I told her. I—I just wanted to tell somebody about those things. Thinking—oh, I don't know. That talking about them would get them out of my mind. A—a man once told me it was good to spill things out. That when you're upset it's a mistake to bottle things up."

"It can be," Clay Arnold said. "We think it can be. That talking things out is—"

He looked into her eyes, looked at her face. What he saw in her eyes, in the tightening of her face, stopped him.

" 'We,' " she said. "You said 'we,' didn't you? And a few minutes ago when I asked you if you read faces you said you looked at people. And then, 'It's part of my—' and didn't finish. Part of your what, Mr. Arnold?" She looked at him intently. She said, "Your job? Was that what you were going to say? Or—no, 'job' wouldn't be right, would it? 'Profession.' That's the word, isn't it?"

He did not answer. He turned toward her, and his fingers left Toby's sleek coat.

She put both hands on the sofa beside her, as if to push herself up from it. But after a second her hands became fists and she turned to look directly into his face.

"And 'mister' isn't the right word either, is it? The right word is 'Doctor,' isn't it? *Isn't* it?"

Unexpectedly to her, the wide smile—the smile which

was more grin than smile—split his tanned face. And, not so unexpectedly, he nodded his head.

"Yes," he said, 'Doctor is the right word, Carol. Clay Arnold, M. D., is the way it reads. Practice limited to psychiatry, if you want the rest of it."

"You slip in the back door, don't you, Doctor? Sidle in? Sneak in?"

"No."

"Because Maude Hudson pushes the door open a little way for you. That's the way it is, isn't it? Says, 'Find out if the poor thing's crazy, that's a good doctor.' It comes to that, doesn't it?"

"No," he said. "Oh, I don't know what may have been in dear Maudie's mind. But I'm not cadging for patients, Mrs. Sanders. I've got all the patients I can handle. Resort town like this—people with plenty of money and nothing to do that needs being done—oh, there's plenty of call on psychiatrists. Plenty of need for them."

"Plenty of money for them, too."

"Yes. Oh yes, the fees do come in. No denying that. And thirty-forty miles from here there's a clinic, and I go there twice a week, Mrs. Sanders. And there aren't any fees in that." He was no longer smiling. "I'm a doctor, Mrs. Sanders," he said, and spoke slowly, spacing the words out. "The way Isaac Strom's a doctor."

She repeated the familiar name.

"Yes," he said. "I studied under Dr. Strom. None of us knows as much about the mind as we'd like to, Mrs. Sanders. Isaac Strom knows more than most of us. A lot more."

"I suppose Maude told you I was a patient of Dr. Strom's? Several years ago?"

"Yes," he said. "Maude was very full of information this afternoon." He broke off and looked up at the ceiling. "Very full," he told the ceiling. He looked again at Carol Sanders.

"None of which"—he said, and again spoke slowly—"none of which makes you a patient of mine. I'm a Saint Bernard who brings lunch across a road to a beach. And lies on a chaise beside a very pretty young woman. A pretty young woman who's been badgered."

"Who *thinks* she has. Who has—how does it go, Doctor? 'Systematized delusions'? Something 'ascribed to the supposed hostility of others'? That's the definition of paranoia, isn't it, Doctor?"

"A definition," he said. "One from a dictionary. We don't put names to things about the mind as much as we used to. But that's a definition. Of a mental disorder you haven't got. Never had."

"You met me early this afternoon," Carol said. "After you'd been told a lot about me. You're very quick with diagnosis, aren't you?"

"Reasonably," he said, and then he smiled again. "Also—I was a little late this evening. People are prompt here. I was late because of telephone calls. I said that, didn't I?"

"Yes, you said that."

"One of the calls," he said, "was to Ike Strom in New York. Dr. Strom says you're one of the sanest young women he's ever come across, in his practice or anywhere else. He says you overworked a few years ago and got the jitters. And got over them." He paused and smiled again. "And to give you his best," Clay Arnold added. "Sounds very fond of you, young woman."

"A consultation?" she said. "But you're not my doctor. You just said you aren't my doctor."

"No," he said. "Just a Saint Bernard."

His long fingers went back to Toby. Toby had gone to sleep, but he wakened enough to purr.

"This man at the restaurant," Clay Arnold said. "This acquaintance you made when you and he worked in the same office. True or false, Carol?"

She looked across the room for several seconds before she answered. Then she said, "You're not my doctor."

He did not answer that. He merely looked at her and waited.

"False," she said, finally, and her voice was very low. He

( 158 )

leaned a little toward her to hear her words. "A police detective from New York," she said, her voice still low. "The one who came around to see me when—when my husband died the way he did. His name isn't Jenkins. His name is Bronson. I think he followed me down here. Because he thinks my husband didn't jump out a window. Because he thinks —this detective thinks—I pushed Ben out the window."

He did not look at her. He looked down at the long sleek cat and again began to stroke the cat. But Toby had had, for the moment, enough of stroking. Toby got up and arched his back and went to the end of the sofa, out of reach, and curled into a knot of cat. Clay Arnold turned toward Carol, and for a moment he merely looked at her. When he spoke, he spoke very slowly and quietly.

"You went over to this detective's table after you recognized him," he said. "Went very abruptly. To accuse him of following you down here? Of annoying you on the way down?"

"Yes."

"What did he say? Did he admit he had?"

"Of course not. He said he was on vacation or leave or whatever the police call it. That he was going down to Marathon to fish. But, he's wearing a gun. When he bent to sit down at the table his jacket bulged apart a little and I could see the gun under it. And a holster and straps to hold the holster."

"New York policemen have to carry their guns all the time," Clay said. "Whether they're on duty or off duty. At least, I've heard that. When I lived in New York. Interned in psychiatry there. Under Dr. Strom."

He took a cigarette pack out of his pocket and tapped two cigarettes to protrude from it and held the pack out toward her. She shook her head. He took a cigarette and lighted it. He looked at the glowing end of the cigarette for some seconds. Then he turned back to her.

"You say he thinks you killed your husband," Clay Arnold said. "Did he ever tell you that?"

( 159 )

"Not in words. Tonight—tonight I said he thought I pushed Ben out the window and he said he didn't think that. But he does." She had been looking straight ahead as she spoke. She turned to the man beside her. "You don't have to say things in words," she said.

"No," he said. "You don't have to say things in words. Why do you think he thinks you killed your husband?"

She did not speak for a moment. Again he held a cigarette out to her and this time she took it, and he snapped his lighter for her.

"Ben and I were alone in the apartment," Carol said slowly. "I was in my own room, getting ready to go to a party. I told Bronson that, but he didn't believe me."

"Did he say he didn't?"

"No. Oh, he was polite. Talked about having to ask a lot of questions for the record. But he didn't believe what I told him. He thought—oh, I don't know how he thought I'd done it. Opened the kitchen window, maybe. Said something like, 'Ben, look down there.' And pushed him when he leaned out the window to look where I pointed." She drew on her cigarette. "I don't know what he thought," she said. "What he thinks now."

"I talked to Dr. Strom for quite a while," Arnold said. "Interrupted him, probably. He had a patient with him, anyway. One of the things I asked was about your husband. Your husband had a brain tumor. Did you know that?"

"Yes," she said. "Anyway, Detective Bronson told me that. That it had showed up in the autopsy."

"Yes," Arnold said. "He would have had to have an operation. Brain surgery. And Dr. Strom wasn't too hopeful about the results. I suppose he didn't tell your husband he wasn't hopeful. But, as you just said, you don't always have to say things in words. And people are afraid of surgery. Particularly brain surgery." He paused and drew on his cigarette. "Oh," he said, "with reason. Even when the surgeon's as good as Strom is. Your husband wouldn't have been the first to kill himself rather than go through that kind of operation."

"He may just—just have fallen. Leaned out too far and—I

don't know. Got dizzy and fallen. Would this—this tumor have made him have dizzy spells?"

"It might have. Did he have them that you know of?"

"No. Oh, he may have had them and not told me. There were, I guess, a good many things he didn't tell me. He didn't tell me about this—this awful thing in his brain. I was his wife and he didn't tell me."

"Some are like that," Arnold said. "Carol—"

For a moment he did not go on. He drew on his cigarette and did not look at her. Then he ground his cigarette out in an ash tray and did look at her.

"Did you love your husband?" he asked her and then, looking into her face, said, "I know it's none of my business. You don't have to tell me that. I'd—it's merely that I'd like to know."

She did not say anything for almost a minute. Then, looking at him, she said, "Because you're my doctor? But you're not my doctor."

"No," he said. "No." He shook his head and then, again, said, "No."

She continued to look at him. Then she said, "Of course I loved him." She put her own cigarette out, slowly, very carefully. While she did that she looked only at the cigarette. While she still did not look at him, looked only at the cigarette she was so carefully crumpling, she said, "Anyway—" The word was a drifting word; it drifted into nothing.

He did not say anything, but she could feel him waiting.

"At first," she said, and did not look at him, "I loved him very much. We loved each other very much. I'm sure of that. But the last year or so I—I don't know. It changed, somehow. Didn't feel the same any more."

"That happens," Clay Arnold told her. "Sometimes there's a reason we can get at. Sometimes there isn't. Did he change? Was that it?"

"Partly, I think. He—he began to seem far away. Off somewhere and looking at me out—out of somebody else's eyes. As if, almost as if, he didn't know who I was. And sometimes he was irritable. As if he did know who I was and didn't like who I was." She stopped and looked at him. "You are being a doctor, aren't you?" she said. "You're not my doctor, but you act as if you were my doctor."

He merely shook his head, rather quickly. Then he said, "Did you tell anybody about this? This—estrangement? A close friend? Anybody?"

"No." Then she looked at him with a kind of surprise. "But now I've told you. And you're somebody I hardly know at all. Why did I do that, Doctor?"

He shrugged his shoulders slightly. He said, "Probably because I asked you to. Perhaps because you've for a long time wanted to tell somebody, and I—turned out to be handy."

"If I had told somebody Ben and I were—oh, what they call drifting apart—this detective might have found out about it. It might have made him suspect me. Is that what you're getting at?"

"Perhaps," he said. "Perhaps that might have entered into it." He smiled again, but this time the smile was only a faint, just perceptible, movement of the lips. "Perhaps there were other reasons."

Then, abruptly, he stood up. He stood in front of her and looked down at her.

"Have you got something to make you sleep?" he asked her.

"Yes."

"Take it. Maude was right. You are tired. You need rest. Will you take whatever it is? What is it, by the way?"

"Nembutal. It says three-quarters."

"Take two of them. Will you do that?"

"Yes, Doctor."

He said, "Good, see that you do," and sounded, suddenly, like a doctor she had been taken to when she was a child.

"And," he said, "lock yourself in. Do you lock doors?"

"Here," she said. "Here I lock doors."

"How many doors are there?"

She tapped her fingers, counting. She said, "Three. The one in front and the one to the carport and the kitchen door." She paused for a moment. "No," she said. "Four, counting the one to the maid's room, which has a door to the outside."

He nodded his head. Then he said, "Tell you what, suppose we check on all of them? Just to make sure."

They checked the carport door and the kitchen door, and both were locked. She showed him the other door from the kitchen, and he opened it and went into the small room with the still neatly made bed. He tried the outside door of that room and came back into the kitchen and pressed in the knob button of the door which led to the little sleeping room.

"There isn't any keyhole to this door," she said, and pointed at the door she meant. "Just a hole in the other knob."

"Yes," he said. "You can push a nail into the hole. Or a skewer or something like that. And release the lock."

"Somebody was in the maid's room," she said. "The night before I got here apparently. Somebody slept in the bed. Did Maude tell you that, too? That, anyway, I'd told her the bed wasn't made up. But that I'd already straightened it, so I couldn't prove—"

"Carol," he said, "you lock the front door after me. And take your sleeping pills. And go to sleep. Will you do that?"

She said, "Yes, Doctor," and went after him to the door and, after he had gone out and while he was walking back to the green Mercedes, made sure the door was locked.

He was right about the fog, she thought, as she watched him walking to his car. The fog's come back.

# 11 ↷

For some seconds she stood at the door and looked out through the glass panel. She watched Clay Arnold swing into the low car and heard its motor start with a roar and watched as it leaped along the driveway and out between the pillars. On the road outside it turned right.

She wanted to go, again, from door to door and make sure that each door was locked. There was almost a compulsion in her to do that meaningless thing. But we just did that, she thought. I will not let uncertainty, intangible fear that I have forgotten, make me do so futile a thing. So crazy a thing. She forced herself to walk to her bedroom door. Toby did not try to come with her; Toby slept in a curl on the sofa. She went into the bedroom and closed the door behind her.

This door could not be locked. There is no need to lock bedroom doors. There ought to be a lock on this door.

She undressed. She went through the routine of bedtime. She took a capsule of Nembutal and put the bottle back in the medicine cabinet. She stood for seconds in front of the washstand and thought, He said two. I told him I would take two. She opened the door of the cabinet and took the bottle out and shook a capsule into her hand and looked at it. She thought, But did I take two the first time? Take two, not one, and forget—forget in seconds—what I did?

I am sure I took only one, she thought. I must be sure

of things. I am sure that all the doors are locked; we went from door to door and made sure about all of them. I can remember we did that; I can see us doing it. I only took one capsule. I am sure of that. My mind's all right.

She took the other capsule and opened the window by her bed and got into her bed and stretched flat in it. The air which drifted in through the window was cool and damp, and she pulled a blanket up over her. The air tasted of the sea. From beyond the road, beyond the wide sloping beach, the sea talked. It did not talk loudly.

My mind's all right, she thought. My mind's all right. My mind's—

She slept. In her sleep she dreamed, but her dreams had no shape. Her dreams were a turmoil in her mind. In one of the dream fragments, the telephone rang and she thought, over and over, I won't answer it, I won't answer it. It will be Ben's voice.

Again it was Toby who awakened her. He did not do it, this time, by standing on her, by touching her lips with a soft paw. He awakened her by yowling somewhere in the house; by screaming somewhere in the house. He seemed to be screaming in great excitement, or in fear.

It was gray in the room. She looked at her watch and saw that it was a little after seven. But it should not be gray in the room. Sunlight should be coming into the room through the open window. Something has happened to my eyes during the night, she thought. Grayness has settled in my eyes. It has settled in my mind. I have to grope in the grayness of my mind to make things come right.

Toby kept on yowling. In terror, she thought, or in fury. I must find out what is the matter with my cat. I must—

Grayness went out of her mind. Fully awake, she swung out of bed. The grayness stayed in the room. Of course! The fog which had begun to form when she went to bed. It was fog coming through the window into the room.

It was chilly in the room. She swept a robe up from the foot of her bed and swept herself into it. At the same time she called, "*Toby! What is it, Toby?*"

He was not, she knew by then, outside her door. He was not, as sometimes he did, yammering to be let in or for her to come out. His voice was different when he did that; it was insistent, but it was softer. Now, ignoring her call to him, he screamed in fear or anger, as a wildcat might scream. Or a hurt cat.

Her fingers slipped on the knob of the bedroom door. She thought, I can't get it open. I can't get it open. But she made her fingers tight on the knob, and the knob turned.

The corridor which led to the living room was almost dark. Her searching fingers found a switch and light came on from above. She ran along the corridor and into the living room and found another switch and lights came on again, this time from the lamps around the room.

Toby was not on the sofa where he had been curled when she went to bed. Toby was not in the room. His frantic yowling came from the kitchen. She ran toward it, calling her cat's name. "Toby! *Toby!* What is it, Toby?"

The door to the kitchen was open and she went into the room and again fingers groped for a switch and light overhead went on.

The cat was standing on his hind legs, his forepaws against the kitchen door. He was screaming at something outside the door.

She went across the room saying, "Toby. Toby." He did not stop screaming at the door; he did not turn to her.

Then there was a man outside the door and the light from the kitchen fell on him. The fog had misted the glass of the door. The man seemed to waver in the fog, began to beat on the door. Then he put both hands on the outside knob and began to shake it. The whole door shook.

He was an enormous man, in the light which streamed down on him. His shoulders were wide—almost grotesquely wide—under a torn blue shirt. He had yellow hair which came down almost to his shoulders, and he had a yellow beard—a scrubby beard on a strangely long face. His eyes were deeply set between high cheekbones and jutting forehead.

"What do you want?" she called through the door. Her voice was very high; her voice was almost a scream. "*What do you want?*"

He made sounds through the door. She could not find words in the sounds he made. He kept on shaking the door. He was yelling something but, again, there was sound, not words, in his voice. It was a high, rasping voice. He began to shake his head, and the long yellow hair swayed about his face. And Toby, paying no attention to her, continued to scream out at the man.

Carol screamed at him too, then. She screamed almost as loudly as her cat was screaming.

"Go away," she screamed at the strange man. "*Go away!*"

He shouted back at her and this time there were words—words somehow blurred—in his shouting.

"Locked," the man shouted at her through the door. "Get in. Got to—"

But then he let go the knob and raised both hands, in fists, and began to hammer at the glass panel in the door and if there were more words she could not, over the beating sound and the screaming of her cat, make them out.

The gun, she thought. Maude made me take a gun. It's— where did I put the gun?

She stood for a minute in the light which streamed down on her from the overhead fixture. The man outside quit beating on the glass of the door and put his hands again on the doorknob and began to try to force it to turn.

She ran then. She ran out of the kitchen and across the living room and down the corridor to her bedroom. I'm sure it's there, she thought. I'm sure that's where I put it. Please, make that where I put it.

She yanked open the drawer of the bedside table and the little automatic was in the drawer. She grabbed it up and held it pointing toward the bedroom door. For a second she stood so, at the foot of the bed, facing the door. I'll wait here, she thought. When he comes in I'll point the gun at him and make him—

Toby kept on yowling at the man outside the kitchen

door and, over the cat's high screaming, she could hear the man's hands beating on the door.

He'll break it down, she thought. He is strong and violent and he'll break the door down. He will come in and—*he'll kill Toby!* I can't let him kill Toby. I can't just—

She ran back again, back along the corridor and through the living room, clutching the little gun. She did not, this time, stop in the middle of the kitchen. She went to the door, and Toby dropped out of her way and quit screaming at the door. But, on the floor at her feet, Toby growled. Fur stood up all over his body and his brown-black tail was bushed.

She raised the gun so that the man should see it. He did not seem to. He kept on trying to turn the knob.

She rapped on the glass with the gun to make him see it. She shouted at him. She shouted, "Go away. *Go away!* I'll shoot if you don't go away."

But I don't know how to shoot, she thought. She told me, but I don't remember. The gun won't go off when it's on safety. There's a little lever somewhere on it. Or a little knob. If it's one way, the gun won't go off. I don't remember which way.

The man outside saw the gun and for a moment stopped trying to force the door and looked down at the gun. Then he shouted something she could not understand and began again to try to force the doorknob to turn. He had, she thought, enormous hands. He could do anything with hands like those.

He began to kick at the bottom of the door while his big hands continued to try to force the knob to turn. The door shook, bounced, with his kicking. He's too strong for the door, she thought. He can break the door down; can break it open. He—

There was a metallic rasping sound and then a sharp snap. The knob on her side turned and the door flew open. She jumped back away from the door and the man started to come through the doorway. He looked down at her and shook his head so that his long yellow hair swayed around

( 168 )

it. He was tall, but not so tall as he had seemed to be when she looked through the misted glass of the door. He looked down at her and then he shook both big hands in front of him. He said, loudly, "Got no right. You've got no right—"

The gun in her hand jerked up; jerked up high. It went off, and the sound roared in the room. And splinters flew from the frame above the door.

For an instant, the man looked down at the little gun. Then he turned and ran out of the house into the patio.

She pushed the broken door closed behind him and tried to lock it. But the lock was broken and would not hold.

He'll come back, she thought. I can't lock him out. He was afraid for a moment, but he'll come back.

She went out of the door into the patio. Beyond the gap in it, she could hear heavy, thudding sounds and thought, He's still running. He's running on the grass. She drew a deep breath. She heard the sharper thudding as he ran on the driveway gravel.

She herself ran across the yielding, too-long grass of the patio and to the gap in the hedge. She stood in the gap and could see him running through the fog. He seemed to waver in the fog. He ran toward the Hudsons' house, and lights went on in that house. The fog blurred the lights.

She stepped through the gap, still holding the automatic but keeping it pointed at the ground. She could see more clearly when she was outside the hedged patio.

An airplane roared overhead. She could not see it through the fog. It sounded very low.

She could see, dimly, a bicycle propped up on the driveway near the Hudson house. The man was running toward it. He grabbed the handlebars and put one leg up to get on the bicycle.

He seemed to balance so for an instant, one foot on the ground, the other raised. Then he fell backward onto the driveway and lay there. The bicycle fell on top of him.

But the bullet hit above the door, she thought. It went into the wood above the door; splinters flew out when the bullet hit the frame above the door. The bullet went over his head. Way over his head.

She dropped the little automatic and began to run toward the fallen man.

The door of the Hudson house opened, and a light went on above it. Then the high floodlight went on. The light seemed to waver in the fog.

Maude Hudson came out of the house into the wavering, grayed light. Then a man ran around the house from the back of it.

Maude ran toward the fallen man and reached him first and crouched down by him. Then she said *"Oh! Oh!"* and the sounds were loud, seemed forced out of her. She stood up and looked at Carol, who went on across the damp grass, her arms hanging down beside her.

"You killed him," Maude said, her voice high, cracking. "You've killed poor Lennie. Why did you kill him?"

The man who had been running around the house reached the man who lay on the drive. The running man was Bill Hudson. He went down on his knees beside the man Maude had called Lennie. He stood up again almost at once.

"He's dead," Hudson said and his voice, like his wife's, was high, shaking. "You killed him. You *killed* him."

He ran back toward the house and into it. He did not close the door after him and Carol could hear him shouting. He shouted, "Emergency! *Emergency*, operator. Get me the police. A *man's been killed*."

Maude stood between Carol and the fallen man and looked at Carol, and Carol stopped walking through the wet grass and stood and felt that she swayed back and forth. She thought, I'm going to fall. I'm going to fall.

She did not fall. She said, in a numb voice, "I couldn't have shot him. I shot over his head. The bullet went into the wood above the door. It couldn't have hit—"

"I told you he would be there," Maude said. "Saturday mornings he comes. To carry the trash cans out to the road so the trucks can empty them. I told you. Told you to leave the door unlocked so he could get in."

Carol began to shake her head, slowly. She said, "No. You

didn't tell me. He tried—tried to break the door down. You didn't tell me anything about him."

"You poor child," Maude said. "You poor, poor child." She looked at Carol and began to shake her head, slowly as Carol had shaken hers. "You didn't know what you were doing. Didn't even remember what I told you about Lennie. Poor, harmless Lennie. He wouldn't have hurt anybody. He—he just wanted to get the cans out to the road. And this was his day to cut the grass. Cut it for all of us."

"He beat on the door," Carol said, in the same numb voice. "Finally he broke the door down. You didn't tell me anything about leaving the door unlocked. He broke the door down."

"He was like a child," Maude said. "Like a child. His mind was like a child's. I suppose—oh, I suppose when he found the door locked he did knock on it."

"Beat on it," Carol said. "Beat on it. He finally kicked it open."

"Oh," Maude said, "he was like a child that way, too. Sometimes. When something came up that he didn't expect —that wasn't the way things ought to be—he—he had tantrums. Like a child. But he never hurt anybody. Never. *Never!* If you'd only left the door unlocked. The way I told you. I did tell you, Carol. I told you to leave the door unlocked so he could get the cans and the lawn mower. Don't you remember?"

Carol shook her head again. She said, "No. I don't remember."

Maude Hudson moved up to her then and said, "Poor child. You poor child. You poor sick child."

She put an arm around Carol's shoulders. She pulled Carol against her. She said, "They'll understand, dear. We'll make them understand. You weren't really responsible. It was just—just one of those things you—you thought were true. Like the car following you on the road. Like—"

"He broke the door open," Carol said. "I'll show you what he did to the door."

She tried to free herself from the arm around her shoulders, but there seemed to be no strength left in her body.

( 171 )

And then she thought, I killed a man. I killed a man. She looked at the man lying on the driveway. He was a big man. His yellow hair spread out around his head. But his eyes were like any other eyes. They were not sunk deep in his head. He looked like a big, harmless man with a long face who was asleep. I killed a man, Carol thought. Killed a—

"There, dear," Maude said. "You didn't know what you were doing."

"I'll show you the door. It's—it's all broken."

"Of course, dear," Maude said. "Of course. It's our fault as much as anybody's. But Bill—Bill insisted I give you the gun. You see—well, we didn't know then, dear. After all those things you said—" She broke off. Then she said, "I should have known better, whatever Bill said." Her encircling arm tightened around Carol's shoulders. "It's cold and damp out here," Maude said. "We'll go into the house and I'll— I'll make us some good hot coffee."

She guided Carol around the body, around the bicycle which had fallen with the man. Carol's body felt numb, as her mind felt numb. I killed a man, Carol thought. I killed a man. I killed a man she says was like a child. She let herself be led into the green house.

Hudson was sitting at a telephone in the living room. He stood up and spoke rapidly, the words chipping out. He said, "They're on their way. And I called Clay and he's coming over." He said this to both of them. But then he looked at Carol and said, "What did you do with the gun? What did you do with it, Carol?"

"I don't know," Carol said. "I—I think I dropped it when I saw him fall. I think that's what I did. Outside, somewhere. When he ran and I—"

She did not finish. She stood and shook her head slowly from side to side.

"I didn't mean to fire it," she said. "I thought it was on safety. No, I didn't know which way it was."

Her voice was so low that she could hardly hear herself speaking.

"I can't hear you," Bill Hudson said. "What did you say?"

( 172 )

"Leave the poor child alone," Maude said. "She doesn't remember, Bill. Doesn't even remember I told her about Lennie's coming."

Carol could see her shake her head, quickly at her husband and Bill said, "Sure. Sure, Maudie," in answer.

"You just sit down, dear," Maude said, and moved to Carol and put both hands on Carol's shoulders and pushed her down into a deep chair. "Just sit and rest. I'll make us some good hot coffee."

She went out of the room toward the kitchen. And, apparently from a long way off, a siren sounded.

Carol sat with her hands in her lap. She looked across the room at nothing. I killed a man. I killed a man. I—

There was the sound of a car's engine outside the house. The sound ended. It had been a heavy, powerful sound. Carol could hear Maude running water in the kitchen; could hear the faint click of metal against metal. She uses a percolator, Carol thought. I killed a man. He is lying outside on the drive in the fog. But I shot above his head. The bullet went into the top of the—

The front door opened and Clay Arnold came into the room. He wore slacks and a yellow polo shirt, but this time he had a light windbreak over the shirt. He had a small black bag in his hand when he opened the door. He put it down on the floor just inside the door.

"Yes," he said, "Lennie's dead. Went through his heart, I'd guess. Nicked his heart, anyway. How—?"

"She thought he was trying to break in," Hudson said. "She'd forgotten to leave the door unlocked. She thought he was going to hurt her. She—well, she says she didn't mean to hit him. Meant to shoot over his head."

Clay Arnold looked at Carol and his eyes narrowed, and the little crease came between his eyebrows. He said, "Is that the way it was, Carol?"

"I didn't mean to fire at all," she said and he had to lean down toward her to hear her. "It just went off. It was pointed up over his head. The bullet—the bullet hit above the door."

"You only fired once?"

"Yes. Yes. I killed him, didn't I?"

"He's dead," Arnold said. "How did you happen to have a gun, Carol?"

"Maude gave it to me. She said everybody here had guns."

Clay Arnold said, "Oh," with no inflection in his voice. And Maude Hudson came into the room carrying a tray with cups and a silver coffee pot on it.

Carol's hand shook so that the cup rattled against the saucer. A little of the coffee spilled into the saucer. She held the cup in both hands and lifted it slowly, very carefully. It still shook when she held it in both hands. It seemed to her to shake with the sound of the approaching siren, which now was very close. Then the siren was a scream, just outside. Then it stopped.

She put the cup down carefully in the saucer and, after it was there, she looked at it, not at any of the people in the room. But she knew that all of them were looking at her. Then, between her and the coffee cup, there was a hand and a pack of cigarettes with a cigarette protruding from it. She looked up and Clay Arnold nodded his head at her, and she took the cigarette and heard the click of a lighter and saw the flame. It wavered in front of her cigarette but then it steadied, and she drew smoke in. For an instant, it seemed to dizzy her.

There were sounds from outside—the sounds of men talking. She could not make out any words. Bill Hudson went across the room, quickly. It was, she thought, as if he were being jerked across the room. He opened the door and went out. He stopped just outside the door. Then, his voice loud, he said, "She shot him, Felix. The poor crazy kid shot him."

A man—was it Felix Sanders's voice? She could not remember how his voice sounded—said, "Jesus Christ," and then, "Why the hell?"

"She says he tried—" Bill Hudson said, but then another man, a man whose voice was low and heavy, said, "O.K. Let's get inside."

Hudson came back into the room and, after him, a heavy

man in slacks and a checked sports jacket. A policeman in uniform came after him and then Felix Sanders. Sanders was wearing a beach robe over pajamas. As he came into the room, Sanders ran his right hand over his hair, smoothing it down.

The heavy man nodded his head to Maude Hudson and then to Carol. He said, "Morning, Doc," to Clay Arnold. He said, "He's dead, all right."

"Yes," Arnold said. "He's dead, Captain. Got him in the heart, I think."

"Doesn't seem to have bled much," the heavy man said.

"Internally," Arnold said. "Pericardial sac, probably."

"Shot from in front, you'd say, Doctor?"

"Yes."

"From close?"

"Look, Captain," Clay Arnold said. "I just made sure he was dead. Not a contact wound. Your pathologist will find out the rest of it."

"Sure," the heavy man said. "Sure, Doc." He looked around the room. He said, "All right. Who's going to tell us about it?"

It was Maude who answered. "She says he tried to break into the house," Maude said. "She'd forgotten I told her to leave the door unlocked so he could take the trash cans out. She didn't know who he was, Captain Larsen. She—"

"This lady here?" the heavy man said, and indicated Carol with a movement of his head.

"I'm Carol Sanders," Carol said. "Ben Sanders was my husband. He was Maude's brother. And Felix's brother. And—"

"Know the family," Captain Larsen said. "Heard about you, Mrs. Sanders. Right old Lennie tried to break in?"

"Yes," she said. The numbness won't go out of my voice, she thought. It—I sound as if I were just repeating things I'd learned by heart. "He beat on the door. Kicked at it. Shouted things at me I couldn't understand. And finally kicked the door open. I didn't know he was supposed to come in and—and carry out the cans. Nobody—"

( 175 )

Maude said, "Carol. Carol dear." There was resignation in Maude's voice. There was something that sounded like pity in Maude's voice.

"All right, Mrs. Hudson," Larsen said. "Let Mrs. Sanders tell what happened. O.K.?"

"Of course, Captain," Maude said. "Of course. She—she hasn't been well, and—"

"Just let her tell me," Larsen said. "Kicked the door open, you say, Mrs. Sanders? Beat on it? Waked you up, maybe?"

"My cat waked me up, I think," Carol said. "He was screaming at something. Or, I thought, was being hurt. It was after that I heard the pounding and—"

She stopped. She picked the coffee cup up and again it shook in her hand. She drank what was in it. She thought, I had a cigarette. What did I do with the cigarette?

"Go right ahead," the heavy man said. "In your own words."

His voice was patient.

Clay Arnold held a cigarette pack toward her again, and she took the cigarette which protruded from it and the light he gave her.

"Your cat waked you up," Larsen said. "Then?"

She told him what had happened and he said nothing, but frequently nodded his head.

"—And Maude ran out of her house and said his name was Lennie and that he was dead, and that I'd killed him."

Larsen said, "Hmmm." He said, "Seemed to be making out all right until he started to get on his bicycle?"

"Yes. I thought so. He—he ran across the grass. I thought he was all right."

Larsen said, "Hmmm," again. He turned to Clay Arnold. He said, "You think the bullet hit him in the heart, Doc?"

"Yes," Arnold said. "I think it did."

"Thing is," Larsen said, "he'd have died right there, wouldn't he? I mean, where he was shot? In Mrs. Sanders's kitchen?"

Clay Arnold lighted a cigarette of his own before he answered. He didn't hurry the answer. He did not look at Carol, although she looked up at him.

"Well," Arnold said, "it depends on the nature of the wound, Captain. Generally, a heart wound is—pretty quick. But there've been cases when a victim ran after he was shot. Even climbed stairs. It's in the literature. Dr. Walker'll be able to give you a guess after he's had a look. Good man, Clyde Walker is."

"Sure," Larsen said. "Sure, Doctor. But for now—he could have walked, maybe run, from Mrs. Sanders's back door to where he is now? With the bullet in him?"

"Yes. It's possible."

Larsen turned to the policeman in uniform. He said, "Tell you what, Ted. You go look at this door, huh? And see if there's any sign of a bullet in the wood above the door? Only, don't try to dig it out if there is. Huh? And have a look round for an automatic Mrs. Sanders dropped. You did say it was an automatic, didn't you, Mrs. Hudson? This gun you gave Mrs. Sanders here?"

Bill Hudson answered that. He said, "Thirty-two automatic, Captain."

"Thirty-two automatic," Larsen told the policeman named Ted. Ted said, "Right, Captain," and went out the door. He reappeared in it almost at once. He said, "Detective Bronson's out here, Captain. Want I should tell him—"

"Tell him to come on in," Larsen said, and Ted got out of the doorway and Bronson came through it.

"You," Larsen told him, and grinned at him, "are supposed to be halfway to Marathon, Larry."

He did not wait for Bronson to answer. He turned to the others in the room and said, "This is Detective Laurence Bronson, folks. From New York. Used to work on the same squad with him before I decided, What the hell, it's too cold up here. And—"

Carol stood up, her movement quick. As she stood she brushed against the table by her chair, and the cup on it rattled in its saucer again and began to slide as the table

( 177 )

tilted. Clay Arnold shot a hand down and caught the swaying table. He checked the slide of the cup and saucer.

"But aren't you the man—?" Maude said, her voice loud. "The man in the restaurant last night? The one—"

"Yes," Bronson said. "I was in the restaurant last night."

"But she said—" Maude said and looked at Carol, who was standing straight in front of her chair; who was looking at Bronson.

"I said he was somebody else," Carol said. "Made up something about him." She flicked a hand toward Maude Hudson, as if to brush her away. For seconds she merely looked at Bronson and he looked back at her.

"So," Carol said, "you're still following me, Mr. Bronson. And now—now you've really caught up with me, haven't you?"

The dullness had gone out of her voice. It was a sharp, clear voice. It was rather high.

Bronson shook his head. He said, "No, Mrs. Sanders. I'm not still following you. I never was. I told you that."

"And lied when you told me that."

He shook his head again. He said, "No."

"Look," Captain Larsen said, "I don't get this. Larry comes through here every couple of years. He gives me a ring. We have maybe a couple of drinks. What's this about his following you, Mrs. Sanders?"

"She thinks somebody followed her out of New York," Bronson said. "In a big car with red paint on a fender. She thinks I was in the car, following her."

"Now," Larsen said, "why the hell would she think that?" He looked at Carol. He shook his head. He said, "Lady, you must be sorta nuts. If Larry here'd been following you you'd never have known anybody was. Also, why the hell would he?"

"To frighten me," she said. "He thinks I killed my husband."

Larsen looked quickly at Detective Bronson.

"No," Bronson said. "I don't think she killed her husband. I think he killed himself. I've told her that." He turned toward Carol. There was a half smile on his face. "Doesn't

( 178 )

seem to do much good, does it?" he said to her. "You ought to listen to people, Mrs. Sanders."

"She imagines things," Maude said. "The poor dear. It's part of—" She stopped with that. She shook her head sadly. Then she said, "Poor dear Carol."

"Go on," Carol said. "Why don't you go on and say it? Part of my being sick. That's what you mean, isn't it? Being crazy-sick."

"Take it easy, Carol," Clay said. "You're not sick."

"There's a man dead out there," Carol said, and her voice was high. In her own ears her voice sounded like a scream. "A man I killed. Because I've got the crazy idea people are trying to hurt me. Because I forget I've been told he's merely a man who comes to collect the trash and I should leave the door unlocked for him. Because—"

"Take it easy," Clay Arnold said again. He moved in front of her and put both hands on her shoulders. He pushed her down toward the chair. For a moment she resisted. Then she let herself sink into the deep chair. She put her hands up and covered her eyes with them.

"This," Captain Larsen said, "I don't get. You get it, Doc?"

"Part of it, perhaps," Clay said. "Not all of it. While she was driving down here from New York a number of things happened to her. Strange, baffling things. Harassing things. She told Maude about them, didn't she, Maude? And Maude told me. Didn't you, Maude?"

"Because you know about such things," Maude Hudson said. "About delusions of—is it of persecution? There's a name for it, isn't there Clay? Para-something."

"Paranoia," Clay said. "Yes, we call the delusion that people are hostile, are persecuting, 'paranoia.' It's handy, sometimes, to have labels to put on things." He paused. He looked from one to another of those in the room, but not at Carol, huddled in the deep chair with her hands over her eyes. He was looking at Felix Sanders when he spoke again. "But it has to be a delusion, of course. Not something that actually is real."

"Sure," Felix Sanders said. "But these things that hap-

( 179 )

pened to Carol. They were crazy things, weren't they? Things that didn't have any point to them?"

"You know about them," Clay said. "Maude told you about them, I suppose? The way she told me about them. Or did Carol tell you?"

"Maude," Felix said. "Sure it was Maude. She—hell, Clay. We don't have secrets in the family. And Carol's part of the family, isn't she? If she needs looking after, we look after her. Needs help, we see she gets it."

"Of course," Clay Arnold said. "I'm sure you'll see she's taken care of, Felix."

He stopped because somebody was knocking on the door. Larsen, who was standing where he could see through the glass of the door said, "Come on in, Ted."

The uniformed policeman came into the room and in the doorway stopped and looked behind him, and down. An automatic pistol dangled by string from his right hand, but he was not looking down at that.

"This funny-looking cat, I guess it's a cat," Ted said, "it followed me over. Got out when I pushed the door open and—"

Ted stood with his feet a little apart. Tobermory came between them and stopped and said, loudly, anxiously, "Yow? Ow-ow-wow-ow?" He looked around the room. He repeated, even more loudly, what he had said before.

"Toby," Carol said. "Here, Toby."

He went there and sat on the floor in front of her and looked up at her. She said, "All right, Toby," and he jumped to her lap. She put the hands which had covered her eyes on her cat. "Everything's all right, Toby," she told her cat, and her voice was low again, and steady. "You're safe now, Toby," she told the cat who curled on her lap.

Everybody looked at the cat, except Clay Arnold. He looked at Carol.

"So, Ted?" Captain Larsen said.

"Somebody pushed the door in, all right," Ted said. "Kicked it and yanked at the knob hard enough to break the lock. Guess it was poor old Lennie. He had strong hands."

"Yes," Larsen said. "I've seen his hands. The doorframe, Ted? Above the door?"

"Banged up," Ted said. "Like somebody'd hit it with a hammer, maybe. Or, sure, like a bullet had smacked into it. Only there ain't no bullet now, Captain. If it was a bullet it kept on going."

"Look like a bullet hole, Ted?"

"Could be," Ted said. "Round sort of hole like a bullet could make. Only it's all spintered up, Captain. More of a nick in the edge of the wood—outside, that would be— than like a hole. One thing sure, there's no bullet in the wood now."

"The automatic?"

"In the grass outside the gap in the hedge around the patio. I didn't touch it, Captain. Just looped a piece of string around it."

"Fine," Larsen said, and took the automatic by its butt and smelled the muzzle. He said, "Yep. Been fired, all right."

He put the little gun on a table. He looked around the room. His look stopped at Bill Hudson.

He said, "You and Mrs. Hudson heard the shot, Mr. Hudson? Almost have had to, right in front of the house."

"Yes," Hudson said, and Maude said, "Bill thought it came from behind the house and went out that way. But I was pretty sure—"

"Yes," Larscn said. "You went out the front door, as Mrs. Sanders said. Mr. Sanders? You and your wife hear the shot?"

"She did," Felix Sanders said. "She woke me up."

"The shot itself didn't wake you up?"

"No, Captain. I'm a heavy sleeper, people tell me."

Larsen merely nodded his head to show he had heard. He looked at Bronson and, just perceptibly, raised his eyebrows.

"I wonder," Bronson said, in a very quiet voice, "whether any of you heard more than one shot?"

# 12

Bronson's question dropped heavily in the room. Carol looked around at the others and thought they were all, quickly, as if in surprise, looking at one another. She looked at Bronson, and could not see anything in his quiet face.

"More than one shot?" Felix Sanders repeated. "I don't get it, Mr. Bronson."

Bronson did not say anything; he looked from person to person in the room. For some seconds, nobody else said anything.

Then Maude said, "What do you mean, Mr.—" and hesitated and said, "Bronson." Then she said, "Poor Lennie was shot twice, was he?" She looked at Clay Arnold. She said, "Was he, Clay?'

"I saw only one wound," Clay said. "An entrance wound. I didn't make a real examination. Just made sure there wasn't anything we could do for him."

"You only heard one shot, Mrs. Hudson?" Bronson said and, when she shook her head, "Mr. Hudson?"

"Just one," he said. "From the direction of Ben's house."

Bronson looked at Captain Larsen and Larsen said, "Sure, Larry. Go ahead."

"Mrs. Sanders," Bronson said, "after this man Lennie broke the door. After you fired over his head, as you say. He ran? Ran out of the house and through this patio?"

"Yes."

"You followed him. Why, Mrs. Sanders?"

"To see—oh, I don't know. To see if he was all right. And, I suppose, that he—well, kept on going away."

"When you were outside, watching him running toward his bicycle. You didn't hear a shot?"

"No," Carol said. "Just the airplane. It sounded very low. Very loud. Up in the fog somewhere."

"Seven-thirty for Jacksonville, probably," Larsen said. "Turbojet. Usually swings out over the ocean before it heads up."

"It's punctual?" Bronson said.

"Taking off it is, anyway."

"The fog wouldn't have held it up?"

"Shouldn't think so. These are low fogs, Larry. He'd be over the fog in—hell, less than a minute. Probably no fog up north. Will lift here in an hour or so."

"Make enough noise to drown out the sound of a shot?" Bronson asked, and Larsen shrugged heavy shoulders. Then he said, "Maybe."

Bronson looked around the room. He said, "The rest of you hear this airplane?"

"Of course," Maude said. "We hear it every morning. It always comes right over here, for some reason."

"Airport's inland," Larsen said. "Wind's usually easterly in the morning. Swings out over the ocean and—"

The sound of a siren interrupted him. Then the door opened and Vinnie Sanders came into the room—came into the room almost running.

She had a rain cap over her hair and a light jacket over a print dress. The jacket was a pale yellow. But there were splotches on it.

Her lipstick's on straight, Carol thought, dimly. She took time to dress and fix her face. But she spilled something on her jacket. She—

"Somebody's hurt!" Vinnie Sanders said. Her voice was shrill. "The ambulance is out there. They're lifting—" She stopped and pulled the rain cap off and shook her head so

( 183 )

that the long blonde hair swirled. She said, "Who's hurt?"

"Lennie, Vin," Felix told her. "I'm afraid he's dead, Vin."

"Dead?" she said. "Poor half-witted Lennie dead? Did—did somebody shoot him? Was that it? One of the shots I heard. Was that it?"

It seemed to Carol, sitting with her cat on her lap, to become suddenly very still in the room. The stillness lasted only for a second. Then Felix Sanders and his sister spoke at once. Sanders said, "Yes, he was shot, Vinnie," and Maude said, more loudly, "What do you mean one of the shots, Vinnie? There was only one shot. Poor dear Carol fired at him because she thought he was trying to break in and—"

"One of the shots?" Vinnie Sanders said. "Did I say *one* of the shots? Why ever did I say that? Of course there was only one shot." She shook her head again. She looked at Carol. "But how awful," she said. "Poor old Lennie wouldn't have hurt a fly. He—he was just a child. Sometimes he got excited but never *against* anybody. You shot him, Carol? *Shot* him?"

"I shot over his head to frighten him," Carol said, and heard her voice dim again. "I meant to shoot over his head."

"How awful," Vinnie said. "How terrible. It's—why did you think he was going to hurt you, Carol? Or—is it just that you think everybody—"

"Because he was trying to break down her door, Vinnie," Clay Arnold said. "Trying to kick it in. He expected it to be unlocked and, when it wasn't, had a kind of tantrum. As a child might have. Because he was a child, you see. Had the mind of a child—a child of about five or six, at a guess."

"But to kill him," Vinnie said. "Kill him. Such an awful thing—"

"Yes," Clay Arnold said. "An awful thing. I doubt if it was meant—" he broke off. He said, "You've got paint on your clothes, Vinnie."

It distracted her. She looked down at her jacket. She said, "Goodness. I certainly have, haven't I? I always do, however hard I try. I didn't realize this was the jacket I wore

( 184 )

yesterday when I was doing my daubs. But it will wash out. It always—"

She stopped abruptly. She stared up at Clay Arnold. He looked at her for a moment; then he looked down at Carol.

"Vinnie paints," he said. "Very nice things. Boats and wharves and—seascapes, isn't it, Vinnie?"

"Just daubs," Vinnie said. "What a time to talk about it, Clay. With poor Lennie—"

"Sure is," Captain Larsen said. "Sure is, Doc. Hasn't got anything to do with anything I can see. It—"

Bronson flicked a hand at Larsen. He said, "Gouache, Doctor?"

"I think so," Clay Arnold said. "Or poster paints. That's what you use, isn't it, Vinnie? Pigments that dissolve in water?"

Felix said, "You driving at something, Clay?"

Clay Arnold looked at Detective Bronson, and Bronson, slowly, nodded his head. But then, quickly, he shook it.

"Clear things up as we go along," Bronson said. "This matter of the shot. Or, as Mrs. Felix Sanders first thought, shots. You're all sure now there was only one shot?"

"I am," Hudson said. "Damn sure there was only—"

"Wait," Maude said. "You were on the other side of the house. If—if poor Carol had fired twice—it's so easy to do with an automatic."

"Yes," Bronson said. "It is easy to fire twice from an automatic. Close together, these two shots you heard, Mrs. Sanders?"

Vinnie shook her head. "I'm sure now it was only one shot," she said. "I was just—just confused."

"What Mrs. Hudson is suggesting," Bronson said, "is that Mrs. Sanders may have fired twice. Missed once and didn't miss the other time. One shot through the door frame. The other into the man's heart. That's what you're suggesting, isn't it, Mrs. Hudson?"

"It—it just seemed possible," Maude said.

"Tricky guns, automatics," Bronson said. "We both know that, the captain and I. Don't we, Tom?"

Captain Larsen said, "Sure."

Bronson took a step toward Carol, sitting with her cat on her lap. He said, "But you're sure you only fired once, Mrs. Sanders?"

"Yes," Carol said. "I only fired once. I meant to fire over his head."

"Not confused about it at all?"

She hesitated a moment. She looked up at Bronson. She said, "No. I'm not confused."

He said, "Good." He continued to look at her. He said, "There was an odd provision in your husband's will. Came across it when we were still nosing around. You know the provision I mean?"

"About—about psychiatric care?"

"That's the one," Bronson said. He looked around the room, at each of the people in the room. "The rest of you know what I'm talking about?"

"I don't—" Felix said, and seemed about to go on. But Maude's higher voice went over his. "Dear Ben was worried," she said. "About— Carol was under treatment by a psychiatrist before they were married. He thought—oh, he tried to think she was cured. But he couldn't be sure, could he? That's why he had that provision put in the will. So—so she couldn't do anything crazy with the stock. Couldn't hurt the family."

"Oh," Felix said. "That's what you're talking about. I said I wasn't sure it would stick."

"His lawyer," Bronson said. "Man named Curtis. He didn't like it, he says. But he thinks it will stick. Wouldn't, probably, if Mrs. Sanders had blood relatives to contest. But way I understand it, she hasn't. That right, Mrs. Sanders?"

Carol said "Yes."

"This provision?" Clay said.

Bronson told him about the provision in Benjamin Sanders's will. Carol found that she was looking up at Clay Arnold; was watching Arnold's face. His eyes narrowed, and the little line came between his eyebrows.

"Funny thing about voices," Clay Arnold said, as if some-

( 186 )

body had been talking about voices. "Telephones change them. Something about the texture changes."

Everybody looked at him. Bronson's own eyes narrowed. Then he said, "Oh. But—" Then he stopped speaking and waited.

"Sometimes," Arnold said, "there's a family similarity with voices. I mean—one sister sounds like another sister. Particularly on the telephone. Sometimes only on the telephone."

"Say," Larsen said, "he's right, at that. Girl I used to call up when I was in New York lived with her sister. Half the time I couldn't tell which one answered. I'd say 'Grace?' The girl I was calling was named Grace. And the sister would say, 'No, Tom. This is Helene.' But, except on the telephone, their voices weren't much alike. Not to notice."

Clay had listened with his head nodding. He said, "Way it happens, sometimes. Carol—"

Carol was looking at him.

"Felix's voice isn't much like your husband's voice was, is it?"

She shook her head. Then she looked up at Felix. She looked away again. She looked at Clay and said, "No, Doctor."

"Have you ever talked to Felix on the phone? Knowing you were talking to Felix?"

"No," she said. She spoke very slowly. "Not that I remember. But Felix was in California."

"I don't get what you're driving at," Felix Sanders said. "Sure I was in California. What the hell, Clay?"

And that seemed to be an answer to Clay Arnold's slowly shaking head.

"No," Clay said. "I guess you weren't, Felix. For a while you were driving that Continental of yours down the Jersey Turnpike. Following Carol's car. With red poster paint —the kind that can be washed off because the pigments are dissolved in water—daubed on a fender. Once you telephoned Carol in her motel room, pretending to be calling somebody else. You knew your voice sounded like your dead brother's on the phone, didn't you? And once you took a screen out

( 187 )

of a window to let a cat out. And once you turned on a car's lights to run a battery down."

"You're the one who's nuts," Felix said. "I was in California. Bill and I were on business and Vinnie—Vinnie went along for the ride. Ask them. Just ask them."

"No point to it," Clay said. "I know what they'll say. Sure you were in California. And I know what Bill and Maude will say. You see—I know what you'll all say. And—what you all tried to do."

"Felix is right," Bill Hudson said. "You've gone nuts, Clay. Half the psychiatrists are nuts themselves. Everybody knows that."

"Debatable," Clay Arnold said, and suddenly the wide smile split his face. But there was no gaiety in the smile, and it went as quickly as it had come. "Oh, you were there, Bill. Seeing a man named Latham. Plant manager. One of Porto-Homes' vice presidents. Telling him that, at the last minute, Felix found he couldn't get away. That you were standing in for him."

"You're—" Felix said, but Clay Arnold's voice broke through his. There was a hard edge in Arnold's voice.

"Maude tried hard," Arnold said. "When she was making the beach picnic for us. Tried to convince me before I met the girl that Carol needed treatment. Tried too hard, Maude did. . . . When I was late last night," Arnold said, "I said I'd been held up by telephone calls. There were two of them. I made them both. One to a doctor in New York."

"Strom?" Bronson said.

"Yes," Clay said. "I called Dr. Strom. And, I called the Porto-Homes plant in California. Afraid I wasn't very honest on that call, Felix. Said I was your assistant here. Said you'd just got back and were short a brief case with papers in it. Said you wondered if you left it in Latham's office. Got through to Latham, finally. Puzzled as hell, Latham was. Because, he said, he hadn't seen you for months, Felix. So how could you leave a brief case in his office? Sure, he'd expected you last Saturday but that Hudson had come instead. You,

Bill," Clay said, "didn't leave a brief case either. Latham wanted me to reassure you about that."

"Dear Clay," Maude Hudson said. "*Dear* Clay. You do make up the most—most absurd things. Almost the way Carol does. Nobody will believe any of these things. Dear Mr. Latham—he was just—just confused. Unless—did you really telephone him, Clay?"

Clay Arnold looked at her for a moment. Then, speaking slowly, he said, "You are trying, aren't you, Maude?" He looked, turning slowly as he spoke slowly, at Wilbur Hudson and Felix Sanders. "You all tried hard," he said. "To make a sane young woman think she wasn't sane. To get her to shoot—maybe kill—a man. In the end, to get a court to commit her to an institution for the insane. The criminally insane. Why? Afraid she would sell the stock? And control would go out of the family? This family you set so much store by?"

"What an awful thing to say," Vinnie Sanders said, her voice very high. "What an awful thing." She paused and shook her head and the blonde hair swirled. "Awful," Vinnie said. "*Awful!*"

"Yes," Clay Arnold said. "I think we can call it that. I think that's the right word for what the four of you did. To Carol. In the end to poor Lennie. Why that, Maude? Or was it you fired the gun, Bill?"

"I was behind the house," Bill Hudson said. "I couldn't have—" He stopped.

Maude Hudson did not look at her husband. She did not look at anyone. It seemed to Carol, watching, that Maude Hudson somehow shrank as she stood there and looked at the floor.

"There was something the matter with the gun," Maude said. "It—it didn't go where it was aimed. At his feet. So, so that—I didn't mean to kill him. There wouldn't have been any need to kill him. To really kill him. It was—it was like an accident."

She looked up, then. She looked up at Captain Larsen. "It

( 189 )

*was* an accident, Captain," she said and her voice went high, and shook. "It *was*. We didn't have anything against poor Lennie. Not to kill him for."

"Automatics tend to jump in the hand," Bronson said. "It's hard to aim accurately with an automatic. But the man's dead, just the same."

"It wasn't planned that way," Felix said, and there was strain in his voice and, to Carol, it sounded for the first time like Ben's voice. No, she thought, it's for the second time. "Nobody planned for anybody to get hurt." He looked for seconds at Maude and they seemed long seconds. "Sister," Felix Sanders said, "you sure as hell loused things up."

The low white house was built around a patio, and Tobermory, harnessed again, was hitched to the leg of a chair. The sun was low, but it still reached the patio. Carol and Clay Arnold sat on chaises, their backs to the sun. But the sunlight flowed onto them.

"—because," Clay said, and sipped from his glass, "since you'd missed him—not wounded him, as she hoped you would—there wouldn't have been a case against you. He was trying to break into the house. As, knowing him, she'd been pretty sure he would. But if he wasn't hurt, they'd probably just have dropped it. But if he was hurt, or killed, it couldn't be dropped. And she would have testified she had told you about his being due this morning. And, of course, about the things that happened to you on the way down."

"The preposterous things," Carol said. "The unbelievable things."

"Meant to be," Clay said. "Planned to be. By the three of them."

"Three?"

"Oh," he said, "I suppose Vinnie knew what was going on. Or part of it. But as to helping plan—no, I doubt it. Not the type. It was an intricate plan. Too intricate for Vinnie, I'd think."

"I tell preposterous stories of persecution," Carol said and looked at the lengthening shadow of a palm tree. "I'm told a man is coming to get trash cans and cut the grass and don't remember—perhaps even don't take it in—and shoot the man. A woman with a history of—of mental illness. It might have worked, mightn't it?"

"It might have."

"With a psychiatrist to be told about these preposterous imaginings of mine. Why didn't you think I—I needed treatment? Or, did you? Because they wanted you to think that, didn't they? Wanted to engage you to treat me?"

He supposed that had been the idea. As to thinking she needed treatment—

"Not after I met you," Clay said. "Oh, you'd told dear Maude some weird stories. Consistent, as they were meant to be, with hallucinations. But I don't diagnose at second hand."

"On a beach," she said. "With martinis and sandwiches."

The grin split his face. He said, "As good a place as any, Carol. Speaking of martinis?"

"No," she said, "I'll have to find a room, won't I? Because I'm not going back to that house. And I'll have to testify at proceedings, won't I? Before a grand jury, or however they do things here."

"Yes," Clay said. "We'll find out about it tomorrow. But I suppose so. As for a room—I've got a guest room here. A couple of them, as a matter of fact."

She shook her head.

"The housekeeper sleeps in," he said. "If that sort of thing's on your mind."

She shook her head again and then turned and smiled at him.

"No, Doctor," Carol said. "But staying here would put me under the care of a psychiatrist, wouldn't it? In violation of the proviso."

"I doubt if—" he said and looked at her and the grin reached across his face.

"On the other hand," he said, "I do prescribe another martini. Not as a doctor. Before I start a fire for a steak."

He picked up the tray and glasses and walked away from her across the patio. She could hear a clatter of something against metal; could see him crouch and plug a cord into an electric outlet. Then she heard another sound, which was the clink of ice against glass. He came back, the sun on his face, carrying the tray with the two glasses. He put the tray down on the little table between them. He held his glass out toward hers and the glasses clicked together.

"Peaceful," he said.

"Very peaceful, Clay," Carol said. And then she said, "Who slept in the bed?"

He twisted to look at her. He put his glass down on the little table. He said, very gently, "The bed, Carol?"

"In the room off the kitchen," she said. "The night before I got here, probably."

"Oh," Clay said. "That bed. I don't know. Maude, I suppose. To provide you with another—hallucination. Probably she planned to go back and smooth the bed while you were asleep. So its having been slept in would be another thing you'd imagined."

"And I was tidy," Carol said. "Tidy and saved her the trouble." She sipped from her glass. "And," she said, "they went to so much trouble, didn't they?"

"Yes, my dear. To a great deal of trouble."

Shade from the hedge crept over their heads, a dark curtain. It was not really cooler with the creeping in of shadow. But Carol shivered. She thought the shiver was only inside herself.

"I think," Clay Arnold said, "I'll move us out into the sun."

He stood up and looked down at her. She stood. She smiled at him and nodded her head.

"Yes," she said. "It will be good to sit in the sun again."